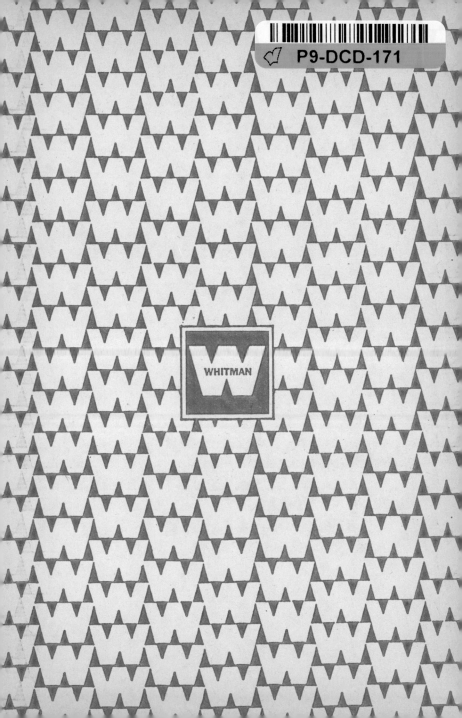

WHITMAN

WAY

OUT

SCIENCE FICTION ADVENTURE FROM
WAY OUT

Edited by ROGER ELWOOD

Illustrated by DAN SPIEGLE

® A WHITMAN BOOK
Western Publishing Company, Inc.
Racine, Wisconsin

CONTENTS

INTRODUCTION

SCIENCE FICTION, since its very beginning, has offered some of everything to lovers of adventure stories: action, suspense, tantalizing glimpses into the mysteries of the future, and—yes—a challenge to the courage of the reader in the face of terror!

Now, with yesterday's science fiction becoming today's scientific reality, science fiction is more popular than ever. Both adult and younger readers are flocking to it at a rate unprecedented in this century, and interest in it continues to grow.

This collection, *Way Out,* offers some of the finest science fiction stories available anywhere. There's something else very special about them: All were written especially for this book—for you—none having appeared in print before.

Among the young people in the following exciting stories, you'll probably recognize someone like you or like one of your friends or classmates. Try to imagine yourself or someone you know in some of these fantastic situations.

In the "pure" science fiction of "The Lights of Mars" by Raymond F. Jones, Jeff Godwin the idealist, heedless of his own safety, clashes with Martin Bailey, who would exploit even a wonder of outer space for the sake of earthly riches.

In "The Face of the Enemy" by Gail Kimberly, refugees from war-torn Earth cannot forget their suspicion and hostility—until they meet the grotesque natives of their new planet.

Not often can laughter be found in science fiction; most of the time the subject is deadly serious. But "Buck and the Gents From Space" by Mack Reynolds is a rare and delightful exception. Guffaws are guaranteed when you read how young Buck, unimpressed by the weird critters that keep landing on his father's ranch, unwittingly launches interplanetary peace!

Definitely of the "serious" variety is "A Matter of Choice" by B. J. Lytle—a story of life on Earth in the next century and of Steven Greenleaf, who manages to become the kind of pioneer that *this* century remembers.

A chilling tale is "Teddi" by Andre Norton, about how bad a world can become when respect for human rights disappears. May there always be a "Teddi" to help life start anew in another world!

"It's So Wonderful Here" by Bill Pronzini is a good story to read—and reread—anytime you think it might be great to get away from Earth and its problems and have an exciting life on some other planet. This one should convince you of the importance of preserving *and improving* Earth—right now!

In "The Little Monster" by Poul Anderson, Jerry Parker is accidentally sent back in time 1,500,000 years. He spends a terrifying thirty hours among pre-men—ape-men, really—who must struggle against beasts of prey for survival. It's just possible, too, that it was Jerry who brought life-giving fire to our fore-bears.

When a computer in outer space makes a big mistake, it's a *big mistake!* In "The Truth of It" by Barry Malzberg, the command robot confesses to Greg that it has made such a mistake and that this space trip will never end. No one on the spaceship believes Greg's story, until. . . .

Believe us—when you picked up *Way Out,* you picked up a book that you wouldn't have wanted to miss! *Good reading!*

ROGER ELWOOD

THE LIGHTS OF MARS

by Raymond F. Jones

THE *Rameses* SETTLED INTO the 10K orbit over Mars, lying in a plane that cut the equator at thirty-five degrees longitude and touched the sixty-third parallel. That brought the ship precisely over Wetzel's Rille.

In the photo observation laboratory, a half dozen technicians made final checks of the camera equipment and waited for the signal from Navigation to begin recording. Two student members of the expedition were on the photo team: Martin Bailey, an engineering student, and

15

Jeff Godwin, an archaeology major. They were assigned to the stereo cameras to photograph the Lights of Mars, a phenomenon that consisted of a cluster of glowing, orbiting spheres that hovered in the depths of Wetzel's Rille.

A red warning flashed on the communication panel. "Thirty seconds," announced Harry Billings, the group leader. "Godwin and Bailey, your power on?"

Jeff nodded. "Power on, sir. Film cartridges loaded."

"Watch the signals. Cameras start at fifteen seconds before visibility."

Jeff put his eyes to the viewfinder and held his hand in relaxed readiness over the trigger grip of the camera. Trying to look casual, Martin Bailey took his own position by his still camera. There was little for him to do except to keep it trained on the target. It was set to record automatically at predetermined intervals, but he could control the length of the interval.

A short beep sounded, and the red light was replaced by a green one. The voices were silent. The only sound was the faint whir of camera motors and the clicking of shutters.

Ten thousand miles below, Mars exposed the long scar that was Wetzel's Rille. It cut a jagged gash nearly three hundred miles across the surface of the planet. The gorge was three to four miles wide and one to three miles deep.

In one of the deepest chasms were the Lights.

"I see them!" Jeff Godwin couldn't restrain himself. "I see the Lights!"

"Watch your camera!" Harry Billings reminded him sternly.

Jeff couldn't help the excitement that boiled within him. They had come forty million miles to see the Lights of Mars. He had seen pictures, of course—color and stereo pictures taken from as close as five miles by previous expeditions. But this was firsthand, and no photos could equal this direct visual experience.

He increased the magnification of his finder until he could make out the separate glowing spheres as the ship slowly positioned itself more vertically over the rille. He jabbed a finger in the direction of the Lights below as he spoke fervently to Martin.

17

"A million years ago—maybe a billion—somebody built those Lights and set them in motion in their orbits, and they've been going ever since. There's nothing like them in the whole universe!"

Martin seemed unaffected by the sight of the Lights. "It's the power you've got to think of," he said. "Just think of the power that keeps them going. There's a secret of power there somewhere, and whoever figures it out and takes it back to Earth can become the richest man in the solar system."

Jeff glanced up at Martin for a moment. "If you could take those spheres back to Earth and harness them to a buttonhook factory, you'd do it, wouldn't you?"

"If there was a market for buttonhooks, I would."

Jeff remained silent as he returned to his viewfinder. During the long weeks of the trip from Earth, he had found that arguing with Martin Bailey was futile. Martin belonged to a breed that enraged Jeff. He was an exploiter—one of those persons unable to look upon any aspect of nature without wanting to mine it, cut it, refine

18

it, or change it into some other form for money-making commercial purposes. Nothing in Martin Bailey's world could be left as it was, to be admired and revered and preserved for generations to come.

Jeff hated all that Martin Bailey stood for, and he found it very hard to restrain his outrage in Martin's presence.

The expedition was the third one sponsored by the Extraterrestrial Archaeological Group of the ancient and respected Peabody Museum. It had taken a long time to convince the Peabody people that there was room for extraterrestrial archaeology, but once the directors were persuaded, they moved swiftly. Mounting three expeditions to Mars in five years was a monumental effort, far different from sending a few diggers to Yucatan or Iran. At the same time, they had sent four expeditions to Venus. They were determined that the exploiters would not get ahead of the scientists in these areas.

Archaeology implies evidence of creatures who have made some effort at organized life. For a long time, it was believed that there were no such

19

creatures on any of the solar planets except
Earth. The idea of archaeology on other planets
was considered self-contradictory.

Then the Lights of Mars were found . . . and
the Valley of Hygirion on the other side of the
planet . . . and the Towers of Suma on Venus.
Suddenly extraterrestrial archaeology was a valid
and respected science. The Peabody Museum
moved to the front, and the government backed
them. For the moment, they were alone. The
Russians hadn't yet entered the field.

The fifty-eight-man third expedition included
six student members, chosen for superior apti-
tude and scholastic ability in the field of archaeology and its branches. This included basic archaeology itself, represented by Jeff Godwin,
and archaeological engineering, represented by
Martin Bailey. Physics, chemistry, anthropology,
and integration science were also represented by
student members.

"It must be pure force field," Martin breathed
as he scanned the Lights through his own viewfinder. "It couldn't be anything else. It will make
every nuclear plant on Earth obsolete!"

Jeff continued watching through his camera sights in silence. Martin's father was president of Intercontinental Power, the biggest power combine on Earth. Power generation had long ago become too complex for individual states to control. It had gradually become national, then international, in organization as world powers were forced to pool their needs and resources.

Martin's father was also one of the biggest contributors to the university and to the Peabody Museum. It was accepted knowledge among the members of the expedition that this was the reason Martin Bailey was a member of the group. His father had twisted arms to get Martin aboard the *Rameses,* and he had put him there for just one reason: to find anything that was commercially exploitable from the historic past of Mars.

Jeff was not alone in detesting Martin Bailey, but everyone knew that the Peabody directors were under constant threat of losing a major part of their support from Intercontinental Power.

The rille and its mysterious Lights seemed to roll slowly beneath the spaceship. The Lights

21

consisted of twenty glowing spheres, each almost four hundred feet in diameter, moving in a complex set of interwoven orbits, like the electrons of a monster atom. The sphere of space that encompassed the orbits was a mile in diameter, and it lay entirely within the rille.

"Don't you think some things ought to stay just the way they were left by the people who built them?" asked Jeff abruptly. "Things like the Taj Mahal, the Pyramids, the Temple of a Thousand Warriors—and the Lights of Mars? They're monuments to the builders. Cannibalizing them is like digging up old graveyards to get gold fillings from the teeth of those who are buried there!"

"That's better than locking the gold-filled teeth in some museum or leaving them in the ground. Gold is pretty scarce; it had better be reclaimed —and if these Lights have recoverable energy sources, I'm going to figure out a way they can be used on Earth."

There might be some token debates about it, Jeff thought bitterly, but, in the end, the great power company would win. It had never yet lost a battle over whose rights should prevail.

Jeff fervently hoped that there was nothing Martin could analyze or find a use for.

The *Rameses* moved progressively lower in orbit, 2K at a time, until the last sweep was made in the landing pattern. They came in over the Lights at an altitude of a hundred miles, then took one more orbit and dropped to the surface at the very edge of the rille, opposite the Lights.

The forty-million-mile voyage was at an end. They were on Mars.

Dr. Allen, the scholarly expedition leader, spoke briefly over the ship's speakers, thanking the flight crew and Captain Moyer. He reminded all expedition members of the precisely timed schedule they had so carefully rehearsed on Earth. Adherence to that schedule now meant success or failure of the expedition, he cautioned.

They stayed aboard that first night. Jeff slept little. The ship had settled in a position that made it possible for him to look directly down on the Lights through the port by his bunk. He had only to raise himself slightly on one elbow, and that

23

was the position he occupied most of the night.

It was like a dream. Surely he would awake and find himself on Earth, not Mars. He had dreamed of the "Red Planet" since he was a child —since he had first read the very old stories among his father's things, in books that had belonged to his great-grandfather. These were the stories of Mars, a strange world, as imagined long before men thought it within the realm of possibility to reach the planet.

That long-ago writer had called the planet Barsoom, and the sonorous name had given young Jeff pleasurable chills down his backbone. The stories told of earthman John Carter, who had been whisked to the planet by mystical means and there fought and lived among Martians in their fabled city of Helium. There he had loved the Martian princess, Dejah Thoris. He had encountered Thuvia, the lovely Maid of Mars, and the scoundrel-genius Ras Thavas, who traded bodies of the old for those of the young.

He saw them all now, out there in the night of Mars. John Carter, at the helm of one of the great Martian airships, saluted majestically, with the beautiful Dejah Thoris at his side.

And he saw the spheres—the Lights of Mars. Even John Carter had not discovered them.

The nearest approach of the orbiting spheres was only three miles away. They swung through their complex paths like miniature planets suspended in space. Their light was not sharp like the glare of sunlight. Instead they glowed, yet the glow was intense; and the depths of the gorge were illuminated by a light that was penetrating but not blinding.

Jeff timed the revolutions of the spheres. Each took about one minute. For an orbit of approximately three miles, that was about 180 miles an hour—not a great velocity but more than he had supposed. He concentrated on a single sphere, until he became aware that it was not repeating a fixed orbit. Each revolution was slightly different from the last. Sometimes the sphere shifted planes. Sometimes it widened or narrowed its orbit.

If they were all doing that, as surely they must be, what an intricate meshing of forces was involved in keeping twenty bodies in constantly

25

changing, interlocking orbits for endless eons!
What guiding force kept them in orbit? What
power kept them in motion?

Within an hour the next morning, the survey
team had laid out the site for the prefabricated
huts that would serve as expedition headquar-
ters. Living space and work space would be abundant, of course, in comparison with the cramped
quarters of the ship, which the staff and crew
had known for so long.

By noon the shells of the huts were up and
being pressurized and tested for leaks. Compres-
sors were already at work accumulating the
rarefied atmosphere of Mars and adjusting its
composition for the earthmen to breathe. By
nightfall the quarters were ready for occupancy.

Two major operations were scheduled for the
next several days. One of these would set up a
radiological laboratory to analyze the radiation
of the Lights. The second was an exploration of
every foot of surrounding territory for at least a
thousand yards with the impact detector. This
was a sensitive electronic device that could de-

tect distortions of ground surface patterns produced by footsteps and other pressures. It could sort out the impacts and graph them pictorially, so that the pressure distortion of footprints in a layer far beneath the surface could be separated from the pressures of overlying soil and debris. Thus it was possible to map the tracks of a man who had walked from his mud and wattle hut to a nearby creek one morning—fifty thousand years ago.

A time calibration was provided by compressing selected samples of soil by known pressures and estimating the degree of compression against a theoretical time scale. It had been successfully used on Earth, at Olduvai Gorge, to track human footprints a million and a half years old—at a depth of forty feet below the surface.

Jeff and Martin were assigned to one of the five impact detector crews, under the immediate direction of Dr. Allen. The work had to be performed in space suits, of course, as did all their activities outside the huts, and it was tedious. Martin fumed, and to add to his ill humor, the temperature controls of his suit were acting up.

27

The detector readings still showed nothing but a solid straight line, after a dozen moves of the equipment. No telltale pressure differentials were revealed.

"We could spend the rest of our lives watching these stupid graphs!" Martin complained.

Jeff sighed, concealing his irritation at Martin's surliness. "If you want to knock off for a while, I'll take care of it until we have to move the equipment to the next square. You ought to report to the technician and get that thermostat in your suit adjusted. It would make quite a big difference."

Martin looked up at the glowing Lights, swinging in their eternal orbits. "The only thing that'll make a difference to me is getting aboard a research ship when they put it in orbit with those Lights."

"You can't do that. The crew was picked before we left Earth. They had a lot of special training for that job."

"I know. But I'm going, just the same. Old man Allen will see it my way—after I talk with him a little bit."

"You could push too far, you know," said Jeff bitterly. "Somebody's going to tell you that you've gone far enough."

Martin laughed. "It isn't going to be anybody on this expedition! If anybody here learns what makes those Lights tick, Martin Bailey's going to be right in the front row."

Silently Jeff turned back to the detector. Moments later, Dr. Allen approached from behind, his suit recognizable by the director's insignia on his arm. "How are you doing, boys? Is the machine working all right?"

"We wouldn't know," said Martin peevishly. "It shows nothing but a straight line—if you can call that working all right."

"It's okay as far as we can tell, sir," said Jeff hastily. "We've found no evidence of any impact distortion."

"I think we may be spending too much effort at too great depths," said Dr. Allen. "We know that Mars has been unaffected by water for at least a million years. Wind action remains, however, even in this light atmosphere. Under these conditions, especially here in the gorge, close to

29

the influence of the Lights, I wonder how much deposit there has been, even in a time span of a million years."

"You mean we might be passing right through something very close to the surface?" asked Jeff.

"Right *on* the surface. I wonder if the builders of these Lights didn't stand and walk on the very surface we're looking at."

"We'll slow the scan to minimum, limit it to the upper half inch, and see what happens," said Jeff.

He made adjustments to the machine, ignoring Martin's boredom and impatience. Then he turned the switches on again, to scan from the surface down to a depth of half an inch, at only one-tenth the rate previously used.

Almost at once, a jagged spike appeared in the trace on the graph paper and then leveled off again. Moments later, another spike appeared a few inches away. Dr. Allen smiled with suppressed excitement. "I think we'll find that's what we're looking for!"

They mapped what appeared to be a print made by a foot consisting of a single pad, triangular in shape, except for smoothly rounded corners. The apex appeared to be the front of the foot. The print measured eleven and a half inches from the base to the apex.

Within two more days, thousands of such prints had been mapped by the five crews. Along with the footprints were paths of vehicles and the impressions of great structures that no longer existed. The entire area below the Lights and on both rims of the gorge had once been the scene of intense structural activity.

At the end of the week, Dr. Allen held a seminar to bring all personnel up to date on the findings. "The best calculations we can make," he said, "show this enormous activity to have taken place about one million years ago, plus or minus ten percent. It obviously had to do with the construction of the Lights. They were built and put into operation at that time and have functioned ever since. To what purpose, we do not know. Our analysis shows also that, like snowflakes, no two orbits are exactly the same. Something keeps the spheres generating new and unique pathways with every revolution."

"And what, do you suppose, does power these spheres, Dr. Allen?" Martin Bailey spoke from the front row. "Of what are they composed?"

"These questions are beyond our present knowledge. We hope to have answers before we return to Earth. Any answer now is pure speculation, but I should like to theorize about the purpose of the Lights, just to stimulate thinking.

"Mars a million years ago was almost exactly like Mars today. Yet then it was inhabited by a race of superior beings. How did they survive? I suspect that they reached a point at which they found survival no longer possible, and they either succumbed—or they left."

"Left?" The word buzzed through the group.

"Maybe they even tried Earth," said Dr. Allen, "and found it inhospitable—or maybe some even stayed. More likely, they moved to some other area in space. But before they left, they decided to build a memorial—a monument. They built the Lights of Mars as a monument to their long civilization here. I'm sure that, somewhere nearby, we'll find their cities and highways."

Dr. Jenkins, the assistant supervisor of archaeology, spoke up. "Is it likely, Dr. Allen, that a people at the end of their resources, desperate to find a new home, would spend the energy, time, and substance required by such a structure as the Lights? Surely they would use those resources in their efforts to leave."

"They were not necessarily in desperation and poverty. They could have planned their departure for generations and could have been rich with the means to accomplish it. The construction of this monument could have been a small portion of their final efforts.

"We may or may not find answers to these questions before we go, gentlemen, but I want you to be aware that you stand beside one of the great monumental works of—I was about to say 'man'—one of the great intelligent races of the universe. Earthmen have left their monuments: the Pyramids, the temples of the Maya, the Taj Mahal, Ankor Vat, but they scarcely touch these Lights of Mars for monumental glory. I only hope that nothing we do, either accidentally or by design, ever lessens the splendor of this great structure."

33

Jeff left the seminar alone. This was his free time, and he was not due to turn in for an hour and fifty-three minutes. He walked over the narrow, metal-grid trails that had been laid out to keep footprints of expedition members from contaminating the surface under the Lights. He walked slowly to a spot directly under the center of the orbits. He bent his head back and watched the whirling spheres on their ceaseless paths.

Barsoom the magnificent, he thought. Here was something truly worthy of John Carter and Dejah Thoris and Thuvia, the lovely Maid of Mars. Here was a titanic splendor, rising in tribute to the imagination of all creatures of all time.

Then he thought of Martin Bailey, with surging fury. Bailey and his kind would never touch this glory. Someway—somehow—he would keep them forever from it.

The nearest orbits were only a few hundred feet above his head. The glowing balls rushing toward him were like suns on their courses, hurtling out of space to destroy him. They brushed the space above him and receded as swiftly as they had come, more like comets, now, than suns.

From all directions their dizzying orbits converged upon him. He seemed lifted up, swirling in the vortex of light that was above him—light that had waited here a million years.

Waited a million years.

Waited for him alone.

It beckoned. It called. It told him that the Builders were not really far away. It told him they would show him great worlds of wonder and light if he would only follow their way.

It was as if there were a voice, but he knew there was no voice. It was a whispering, like the sound of space itself, and he knew, quite naturally and without question, that he had to obey. He had to follow. He had to follow the Builders.

Whoever—wherever—they were. . . .

Dr. Allen was awakened by his assistant at about 2:30 A.M. No one else in the camp was awake, except a routine guard posted on the *Rameses* as a precaution against sabotage by some berserker whose dormant mental aberrations had gone undetected. The guard called the base administration hut, and it was Dr. Jenkins who answered.

Dr. Jenkins roused Dr. Allen and spoke quickly to him. Dr. Allen wakened slowly and unbelievingly. Dr. Jenkins had to repeat his message three times. Then they went to stare out through the hut port that overlooked the Lights.

One of the two jet research ships, which had been parked near the huts, was gone. Jenkins pointed silently toward the Lights.

Dr. Allen couldn't see it at first, but then his eyes became accustomed to the contrasting light and darkness, and he saw the ship. It was in the midst of the Lights, swinging in orbit a short way behind one of them.

Dr. Allen gasped. "Who—"

"Young Godwin. Jeff Godwin."

"I don't believe it! He is one of the most stable members of the whole expedition. He wouldn't pull a fool stunt like this—taking a research ship into the Lights on his own."

"I made a bed check before I woke you. Everyone's accounted for but Jeff."

"I still don't believe it. Let's try the radio."

No one had given any general alarm, but somehow the entire camp was aroused now, and the

whispered fact spread like prairie fire: Jeff
Godwin had taken a research ship into the Lights.

In the radio room, Dr. Allen, still in his sleeping garb, snapped angrily into the microphone.
"Jeff, answer if you hear me. This is Dr. Allen.
You are to return to base at once. Jeff Godwin,
return to base at once!"

There was an intense crackle of static from the
radiations of the Lights. But the radio lines of
the ship were open. Jeff's voice came in, but too
faintly for them to distinguish his words.

"Repeat, Jeff Godwin. We do not read you."

Jeff's voice came in again, just enough strong-
er that they could make out his words. "I can't
return," he said, "unless they send me back from
beyond the Gate. There's no way out of the orbit
until I reach the end, and the end is not here."

"Jeff—is your ship damaged? Is there anything we can do to help you get it repaired? We
must get you down. You'll be out of fuel soon.
There wasn't much aboard the ship."

"I'm not using fuel. I'm orbiting entirely under
the influence of the Lights."

"Use your retros, then!" Dr. Allen ordered.

"Break out of orbit. You should be able to come up to the rim by the base. If you can't do that, coast to the bottom of the rille, and we'll pick you up from there."

"You don't understand." Jeff's voice sounded far away and faintly bemused. "I'm not coming back. I can't, for one thing, but I wouldn't if I could. I'm going on. I'm going to meet the Builders. I may return sometime. I can't tell now. But tell my dad not to worry; I'm all right. Remember how he always wanted to find his great adventure and never did? Tell him I've found mine, and he'll be glad."

Dr. Allen turned from the radio in despair. "It must have affected his mind," he said to Jenkins. "How are we going to get him down? He may be right about being caught in the influence of the Lights and orbiting without power. If that's the case, he could die of starvation up there in orbit."

Dr. Allen and Dr. Jenkins donned suits and went out to the rim of the gorge. Others had preceded them and stood watching the incessant spinning of the Lights. They seemed to be taunting them now, Dr. Allen thought, as if smug in the knowledge that they had captured one of the earthmen who dared to intrude upon the silence of a thousand millenia.

He turned up the thermostat of his suit against the chill that suddenly shook him. He remembered such a chill from his youth, standing in the moonlight before a newly discovered Mayan temple in the jungle of Yucatan. Always, it seemed, a vestige of death hung over these ancient monuments until modern man cleansed and polished them and made them pretty for the tourists to see.

He wondered, half seriously, if there were any truth in young Jeff Godwin's illusion that the Builders of the Lights somehow persisted nearby. He shook off the thought. He was a scientist. He had no right to such superstitions and emotional whims. He had a problem now, too. One of his staff was in danger, his life imperiled by a foolish whim. Somehow they had to break Jeff Godwin out of that entrapping orbit. . . .

He turned back to the base, his mind empty of ideas. Suddenly a flash of motion and a burst of flame crossed the edge of his vision. He looked up with a start. The second research ship was rising, in a long arc, and turning down to meet the orbiting Lights in the gorge.

"Who's in that ship?" Dr. Allen demanded over his suit radio. "Who authorized that flight?"

Martin Bailey, at the unfamiliar controls of the small jet research ship, knew he was gambling heavily. His chances of overtaking Jeff Godwin were marginal, at best, unless he could manage to insert himself into the same orbit, close to Jeff's ship. Collision was only one of the risks. Contacting Jeff and determining what he knew was another risk. Getting back alive was the final one.

But then, he belonged to a family of gamblers. His father had taken enormous risks at every step of his career, and he had taught Martin that the only path to wealth and power was paved with risk.

This flight was a risk that had to be taken. Jeff Godwin had somehow learned something about the Lights that none of the rest of them knew. It could lead to control of the force that powered

41

the Lights. If Jeff Godwin seized that secret ahead of him, Martin would be disowned by his father.

He didn't understand what was to be accomplished by Jeff's flight. He had gathered from the conversations at the base that Jeff's ship was disabled, but Martin didn't trust that word. He suspected Jeff had offered it as an excuse to stay in orbit to complete his observations. All this surprised Martin greatly. He had not supposed Jeff Godwin capable of such aggression. He knew now that he had made a mistake in confiding to Jeff his own intentions.

Martin was an expert pilot of his own private craft, but the research ship was like a clumsy workhorse compared with his sleek and responsive racers. He took the ship once around the sphere of orbits. At the bottom of the gorge, he almost touched the scaffolding of the impact detectors as he shot under the Lights. He spotted Jeff's ship on the upside and moved in close to get into orbit behind him. Then he was over—hovering—dropping—

Down!

He was in orbit, and it was like suddenly being locked onto a track. He felt a momentary panic, but his instruments told him his engines were still working, so he could easily break free if he chose.

Jeff's ship was a few hundred yards ahead. Martin flipped on the radio control. "Jeff, this is Martin. Are you in trouble?"

Jeff's voice held a laugh. "No, but I think you are."

"What do you mean by that?"

"I don't think you want to go where we're going. But I don't think you're going to get there, anyway."

"What the devil do you mean by that? We're not going anywhere, except back to base. They sent me up to see if I could give you a hand. What did you come up here for? What can you learn here about the Lights?"

"You don't understand, do you, Martin? You think I came to find out the secret of the Lights, and you couldn't stand to have me discover it before you, could you?"

"You know what I came for. Nobody's going to get it ahead of me."

43

"You can relax, Martin. What you want isn't to be found here—by either of us. There's something much greater, and you aren't going to find that, either."

"Why did you come?"

"They called me," said Jeff. "They told me I could come to where they are, and I couldn't turn them down."

"*They?* Who? What are you talking about?"

"Listen! Stop your stupid yakking for a minute and listen."

"Listen to what?"

"The voice of ancient Barsoom."

"The voice of *what?*"

"Shut up and listen!"

Martin remained quiet and watched the ship ahead. Jeff's words made no sense at all. Martin wondered if the aura of the Lights had affected Jeff's brain.

It seemed to him now that they were no longer traveling in a circular orbit. Rather, they were rushing through a tunnel of light, gaining speed at a fantastic rate. They followed just one of the Lights, which seemed to guide the way. Beside them, all the other Lights bore through space like guardian angels.

Martin wondered what had happened to the orbits and the sphere of space in which they rode and the gorge of Wetzel's Rille. The base, Dr. Allen, the expedition—where had they all gone? He didn't know. It seemed only that he had been borne along through this tunnel of light for an eternity and that there was an eternity still ahead of him. He remembered Jeff's admonition to listen, and he listened, and in his head he heard the sound of space.

He heard sounds such as he knew no man had heard before—messages of light and wisdom and glory. "The voice of ancient Barsoom," Jeff had said. That was it, Martin knew; the voices of the ancients of Mars. And Jeff was talking, too. He was talking in their language, and they were listening to him.

And what he heard froze Martin's heart. The voices were closing the door on that glimpse of light and wonder that he had beheld. They didn't want him. They weren't going to let him in.

Jeff Godwin was telling them that they must

not let him in. Jeff was robbing him of entrance, here on the very threshold of this world of the Builders. Martin cursed at Jeff and raved and pleaded for admittance.

The voices swelled in bitter denial.

The ship ahead of him seemed suddenly to increase its speed, and the distance between Martin and Jeff Godwin widened swiftly. Martin screamed into the radio: "Take me with you! Don't let them shut me out! Jeff, listen to me! Tell them to let me in!"

Jeff's voice came back with a kind of sadness in it. "Now you know," he said. "Now you know, Martin. You can't come here. There's no room for your kind here. They have a name—Eater of Worlds—that's what you and your father and all your kind are. Eaters of Worlds. You consume everything and give nothing. The Builders have no room for you.

"Tell Dr. Allen I may be back. I don't know whether it will be possible or not, but tell him I'm not afraid. I'm not afraid of anything anymore."

"Jeff! Jeff—wait. . . ."

The distant ship vanished from his sight. It seemed as if it had suddenly speeded up to infinite velocity and vanished into the depths of an unknown universe. Simultaneously the tunnel collapsed around him, barring Martin's way. The ship bucked and rolled. It careened as if caught atop a mountainous wave. The light became a fire that ate at him and through him and destroyed his very cells.

Martin Bailey regained consciousness in the spartan hospital quarters of the base. Dr. Mahon, tho baɜc physiciaii, stood nearby.

"He's coming around," the doctor said. "He's a very lucky fellow. He had no right to survive that crash, but I can't even find any really serious injuries, so far."

Martin focused his eyes. Dr. Mahon became recognizable. Dr. Allen was there, too. The archaeologist touched his shoulder.

"That was a very brave thing you tried to do, Martin," said Dr. Allen. "Trying to rescue Jeff single-handed was a very brave attempt. It was also a very foolish one. You didn't have a chance

47

to get him out of orbit by going in after him. You're lucky to be alive."

So his ship had crashed. That long journey down the tunnel of light? It must have been some kind of illusion. Where it went he would never know.

"Jeff—" he said abruptly. "What happened to Jeff? Is he all right?"

"We don't know what happened to Jeff," Dr. Allen said. "You both were in the Lights for a long time. But just before you crashed, he seemed to disappear. We couldn't locate him anymore. He just vanished. Then your ship burst out of orbit and crashed."

Martin closed his eyes. So they didn't know. They thought he had gone up in the second ship to rescue Jeff. They didn't know he had simply tried to beat Jeff to the secret of the Lights. He was in the clear.

No, that wasn't right, either. He wasn't in the clear. He had found out something about himself. What was it Jeff had said? "Eaters of Worlds," the Builders had called his kind. He cringed at the words. They had an ugly sound.

But maybe he was an ugly human being, too.

For the first time, he sensed what men like Dr. Allen and Jeff Godwin stood for. He knew now why intelligent beings built a Taj Mahal and a Temple of a Thousand Warriors—and the Lights of Mars.

"Dr. Allen?" Martin Bailey held out his hand as the archaeologist turned to go.

"Yes, Martin?"

"I didn't go out there to rescue Jeff Godwin. You've got to know that."

Dr. Allen raised his brows. "What did you go for?"

"I went out to try to find the secret of the power of the Lights before Jeff found it. That's the only reason I came with the expedition—to take that information back to Earth with me."

"I was aware of that," said Dr. Allen grimly. "Your father forced your presence on us."

"But up there in the Lights, I found that wasn't at all what he was after."

"What was he after? Did you find that out?"

"The Builders called him. They invited him to come through."

"The Builders? Come through? To where?"

"The Lights are a monument, but they're more than that. They're the Gate. They are the Gate by which the Builders escaped to—wherever they are. I don't know if it's distance or time or some other dimension of space, but wherever they are, the Lights form the gateway to it."

Dr. Allen sighed, scarcely believing, but knowing he had to believe. Jeff was gone. "I see. And they are still there, watching the Gate from the other side?"

"Yes."

"And we can go through? Any of us can go through to the realm of the Builders?"

Martin shook his head. "Not unless they invite you. They invited Jeff. They rejected me." He hesitated, as if unable to say the words. Then he went on. "They called me an—an Eater of Worlds. They despise my kind."

Dr. Allen nodded slowly. He understood what the Builders meant. Eater of Worlds. It was an apt term.

Martin remained silent a long time. His eyes were closed. The archaeologist turned quietly to leave the room again, but Martin Bailey stopped him once more.

"Dr. Allen, I think we ought to do everything necessary—legislation, guards, whatever it takes— I think we ought to make sure that nobody ever tries to disturb these Lights again."

"I agree." Dr. Allen nodded and smiled suddenly. "I agree, and your influence—and that of your father, if you could persuade him—would go a long way to make it certain."

"I'll persuade him," Martin Bailey said grimly. "I'll make him see it, somehow. I'll make him stop being an Eater of Worlds."

"I hope you do."

"One other thing. When we get back, I'd like to see us propose a monument to Jeff Godwin. I'd like to see this monument officially named Godwin's Lights. Do you think we could do it?"

Dr. Allen touched his shoulder with sudden fondness. "We'll try, Martin. I think it's a very thoughtful suggestion. We'll try to put it through."

THE FACE OF THE ENEMY

by Gail Kimberly

ANOTHER SPACESHIP HAD LANDED here on this planet they had named New Earth.

Chad Reynolds, with his father and two of the other men, stood under the blue gray trees on a hill and watched as the spaceship burned its way down to land on the ferrous-red ground, not five kilos from their own settlement. He wondered who would be in that ship, and, as they climbed into the aircar they had left in a clearing and flew it to the place where the ship had set down amid singed vegetation, he felt tight with fear.

His fears were justified. When they were close enough, they saw that the ship bore the insignia of the enemy. They got out of the aircar and waited.

Three men came out of the ship, squinting their eyes against the unaccustomed brightness of the white sun and holding their hands against the L-guns strapped to their belts. Chad's father swore softly, and the two men with him went rigid. The others stopped just outside their ship. Then they all stared at each other in the hot, bright silence. Finally one of the newcomers held up two fingers in the ancient sign of peace, and the two with him gravely did the same. Chad let out the breath he hadn't been aware he'd been holding.

"This land is ours." His father's voice boomed at the strangers. "Do you understand that?"

The man who had first given the sign of peace answered him in English. "This planet is habitable. We have traveled long and far. We will stay here."

There was uneasy shifting and muttering among Chad's group, and again it was his father

53

who spoke. "How many people have come with you?"

"Twenty-six adults, ten children. And you?"

"Our colony consists of exactly forty-three Americans."

The man standing next to Chad called out, "How are things on Earth?"

The newcomer shook his head heavily and frowned. "We left more than a year ago, but communications had stopped weeks before we escaped. We were the only survivors in our city. Earth must have been destroyed by now."

Chad shuddered. Their group had left Death Valley Central Spaceport right after the first bombs began devastating the eastern states. Other groups were leaving, too, but theirs had been the only one to land on this planet, even though it had been charted by the interstellar explorers and was known to have an oxygen-nitrogen atmosphere. Chad's father, who had been the captain of an interplanetary trader, had hurriedly gathered his family, his crew, and as many others as could be taken into his ship and had blasted off, knowing the holocaust would not end, once it had started. Now the enemy stood before them —the destroyers of Earth, who had sent the first missiles as a prelude to the ravage of the planet they had all shared.

"Why did you start the war?" one of Chad's group asked.

The strangers looked astonished and spoke together in their own language. Then the spokesman answered, *"We* did not send the first missiles. *You* did!"

The three Americans laid quick hands on their L-guns. The three others did the same. The white sun burned down angrily on tho tonoo oceno as the door of the silver ship opened. People filed solemnly out, some leading or carrying small children, and arranged themselves around their spokesman.

Chad's father turned and started back toward the aircar, drawing the others with him. "They might get ugly," he said.

Immediately the stranger called after them. "We come in peace. Will you stay and talk with us?"

"Peace, he says!" one of the men muttered.

55

"Earth destroyed . . . Los Angeles burned to cinders . . . my folks dead . . . and he talks about peace!"

"They want us to help them," Chad's father said. "We've been here longer, and we have more people. Once we help them get settled here, they'll be up to their old tricks again, starting trouble."

The coaxing, accented words came again. "Will you not stay and talk with us?" They turned and saw the three armed men coming slowly toward them.

Chad's father looked worried and conferred with the two other men. Chad looked at the group around the spaceship and noticed a boy and a girl, both about seventeen, his own age, who were taller than the others. Both wore short tunics and sandals. The girl's hair was long and thick, and it glinted blue black in the sunlight. The boy looked angry and was glaring at him.

Then Chad heard his father speaking. "We'll stay, but my son will take the aircar back to our settlement to tell everyone that you're here and to bring some others back to meet you." Then,

56

in a low voice, he said to Chad, "When you get back, tell Mason and Sephton to fly back here. Make sure they're armed. You stay there."

"How about taking some of them with you?" the man next to Chad whispered. "They'd be our insurance that we'd be safe here."

Chad wasn't too sure he liked that idea. He could feel hostility and suspicion in the air, so thick it almost choked him, but his father was walking toward the enemy. He stopped in front of their spokesman, and then he indicated the boy and girl, who had moved away from the group. "How would these youngsters like to go with my son and see our settlement?"

The spokesman looked startled for an instant, before his expression was masked with a smile. "My son, Ling Won, and my daughter, Ti-San," he said.

"Glad to meet you." Chad's father nodded at them. "I'm Lan Reynolds, and my son is Chad. Like to go for a ride in the aircar with him?"

The boy spoke briefly to his father in his own language and then, without waiting for an answer, strode over to Chad. Ti-San had to run to keep up with him. His eyes flickered black fire at Chad as he spoke. "Okay, hotshot," he said in perfect English, "here are your hostages. But we had better get back safely, or I will personally beat your head in!"

The aircar hovered over the crimson beach at the edge of the purple sea. Ti-San's black eyes shone as she looked down, but Ling Won sat stiff, silent, and unfriendly.

"Our settlement's over there." Chad pointed to his left. "We've already got houses built, and we're clearing the land for planting. You'll see it in a minute." He headed the vehicle inland. "It's surrounded by jungle. You probably know that this planet is mostly jungle. We've discovered small animals and fish and birds of different varieties, but we seem to be the only intelligent life here."

Ling Won lifted an eyebrow. "Is *that* what you call yourselves?"

Chad felt his face getting hot. He jerked the lever that controlled the altitude and sent the craft into a climb. He'd shake this guy up a bit.

He guided the car into a loop and climbed again for another, watching Ling Won's face turn white. But after the second loop, Ti-San was crying with terror, so he leveled the aircar and skimmed it over the blue gray tops of the trees.

Ling Won's face was grim, and his hands were clenched into fists. "I don't want to go to your settlement," he said tersely. "Take us back to our ship."

"My father told me to go to our settlement, and that's where we're going."

Ling Won's hands shot out and clutched at the controls. Chad tried to pry them off, but he couldn't break the rigid grip, so he grabbed Ling Won's neck—and then they were struggling, while the craft dipped and shivered, out of control. Ti-San screamed. Chad felt fiery pain as Ling Won chopped at his neck, and he lashed out with his fists at the other's face. Another chop made his head spin so that he had to close his eyes, and when he opened them, he could see the trees surging toward them. He grabbed the control lever and pulled, but then another blow at his neck made everything go black.

Chad lay with his eyes closed, not even trying to open them. His head throbbed with pain. He tried to remember what had happened; then he did remember, and he opened his eyes. He was lying on his back under thick-branched trees, and the boy and girl were watching him from their seat on a log close by. Ti-San had a bruise on her delicate face and one on her bare upper arm. She looked as though she had been crying. Ling Won held one leg stiffly in front of him, and Chad could see that his nose had been bleeding and one of his eyes was blackening.

He sat up. "What happened?" His head throbbed wildly, so that he had to close his eyes until the pain subsided.

"We crashed, of course," the girl said. "We are lucky to be alive." She felt her bruised face tenderly. "What else could happen when nobody controls the aircar?"

"Well, that wasn't my idea," Chad said bitterly, scowling at Ling Won. He tried to stand up, but his head hurt so much that he sank back to the ground. He put his hand up to his forehead and felt raw pain under his fingers, and the

sponginess of congealed blood.

"You must have hit your head as we crashed. It is a very bad cut," Ti-San said. "You were unconscious, so we brought you out here."

Chad felt sick from pain and anger. Ling Won had wrecked the aircar, and there was only one other in the settlement. The colony would suffer from that loss. He groaned, then felt gentle hands lifting his head and gentle fingers pushing something into his mouth. "Here, take this," Ti-San said.

"What is it?"

"The label says it is a pain-killer and an anti-biotic. It is from the first aid kit in the aircar."

Ti-San unrolled a bandage and handed it to her brother. He wound the bandage carefully around Chad's head.

When he was finished, Chad sat up slowly. The throbbing seemed to be going away, but he felt a terrible thirst. "Thanks for the first aid," he said.

Ling Won twisted his lips into a wry smile. "You are of no use in returning us to our people unless you can travel. How do we get back?"

"How should I know?" Chad said. "I told you this planet was mostly unexplored. I have no idea where we are. If you'd kept your hands off things, this never would have happened."

Ling Won's face tightened, and he rubbed his sore knee. "It was your fault, rolling your plane around that way, trying to frighten us. You made me angry. I only wanted to get on the ground again."

Ti-San sounded tired. "Never mind blaming each other. What do we do now?"

"There's one more aircar in the settlement," Chad said. "I guess they'll send it out to look for us when we don't show up."

"But how will they know where to look?" Ti-San asked.

"Well—I don't know. I don't know how far away we got before we crashed." Then he remembered something. "Wait, there's a radio in the aircar—" His voice broke off as he saw both of them shaking their heads. They must have checked the radio when they got the first aid supplies. He got back to his feet in silence and began to pace back and forth across the mossy ground.

63

Finally Ling Won spoke. "My people will think you have kidnapped us. When we do not return, there will be trouble."

Chad thought of his father and the other two men, waiting for Mason and Sephton to arrive. They wouldn't know that the settlers had never been told about the enemy ship. That meant that the three could be held prisoner if he didn't bring back Ling Won and his sister. Right now his father was in great danger, and so was the whole settlement, and Chad didn't know how to save them. He'd have to get back fast, but how?

Well, first he would take care of his thirst. The others were probably thirsty, too, and hungry. Wordlessly, he left the clearing and headed for the aircar lying a short distance away. It lay lopsided, its front rim crushed against a tree trunk and one door twisted off its hinges. He crawled into the front seat and felt underneath for the locker that held the emergency rations. It was open, and it was empty—but it had been stocked with food tubes and vitabars and a gallon tank of water! He poked under the seats and behind the control panel but found nothing. He climbed

64

out and hit the side of the crippled car with an angry fist. Those two! They had taken the food out, along with the first aid equipment, and hadn't said one thing to him about it! Going to keep it all for themselves, probably. He ran back to the clearing.

They were still sitting on the log, watching him as he ran toward them. "Okay," he shouted, "where's the water? And the food?"

Ling Won stared at him coolly, and Ti-San pointed to a nearby bush. Under it, divided neatly into three equal piles, were the emergency rations, with the gallon tank of water beside them. "We did not eat anything," Ling Won said. "We were waiting until you came back." Then he began to laugh, showing his small, white teeth, and Chad felt his anger burn itself into a knot of embarrassment in his throat.

"Shut up and hand me the water, will you?" he said.

They ate the vitabars and sipped the water, and Chad stored the food tubes in the pockets of his shirt and pants. Ling Won carried the water, and they began to walk in what Chad hoped was

65

the right direction, although he wasn't at all sure. After a long time of pushing back the rubbery bushes and ducking under the low-branched trees, they found what looked like a trail. It was a smooth ribbon of ground, where foliage had been cleared away. In one direction, it seemed to lead to a high hill not far away. In the other direction it went on through the jungle. It was this last way that Chad decided to take. "I'm pretty sure it'll lead us to the ocean," he told the others. "Once we get there, we'll be better off. Searchers will find us more easily, and I might spot some landmarks I can recognize."

"Somebody made this path," Ling Won said as he limped behind Chad.

"Animals, maybe. It could lead to a water hole."

"Or maybe this planet has other inhabitants besides the animals," Ling Won said, and Ti-San, walking behind him, gave a little squeal of fright.

"There are no intelligent beings, if that's what you mean," Chad said.

"How do you know? Did you not say this planet was largely unexplored?"

66

"Well, we haven't seen any in the ten months we've been here."

"Maybe they have seen you."

"Then why wouldn't they contact us?" Chad said, trying to sound positive. But he had thought of the same thing, and the settlers had discussed it many times among themselves. It was generally agreed that once the colony was more stable and their food and shelter secure, there would be exploration parties sent out. It didn't seem reasonable that a lush and fertile planet could be barren of all but the lower forms of life.

Ling Won's face showed his disdain. "That is just like your people," he said. "You think you are the only important beings on this planet, just as you did on Earth. Will you kill off all the life on this world, too?"

Chad turned on him. "Why don't you just shut up? Your people were the ones that destroyed Earth!"

"Why do you keep on blaming us? It makes no difference now. Why not admit that your country started the destruction?"

Chad was about to answer, when they heard

67

the sound, coming from someplace close, shrilling clearly over the rustlings of the jungle and over the sudden pounding of their hearts.

Somebody was singing.

At first it was the sound of only a single voice, but as they stood frozen, they could hear another voice join the first, and then another, and then their ears were full of the strange melodies that wove themselves into a weird chorus. For a long time, they could do nothing but stand there and listen, wondering, and then the chorus became a duet and then, again, a solo, and finally that faded into the chirping of a bird nearby that carried the last note of the song away with him on excited wings.

Ti-San moved closer to Chad. She was shivering. "What was it?"

He shook his head and began moving cautiously along the path, straight ahead, in the direction the sounds had come from. Ling Won fell in behind. Ti-San sighed and followed. Soon the bushes thinned, and they could see the red beach beyond. They looked out through their screen of foliage and saw figures on the red sand, some

68

leaping into the breakers, some running along the shore. Nine of them, Chad counted—nine beings that ran on two legs, with scaly skins that matched the color of the purple ocean. Their heads were shaped like the heads of alligators: long-snouted, sharp-toothed. The biggest seemed to be a head taller than Chad's six-foot height, while the smallest were the size of three-year-old children. As the earthlings stood watching, the singing came again, now from one of the small creatures, who ran across the sand toward a bigger one.

Chad was so intent on watching them that he jumped when Ti-Sun touched his arm. Her face was pale and anxious. "They are ugly," she said. "I would like to go home now."

He wanted to say, "Me, too," but, of course, he couldn't. She was looking to him for help, and what could he do? The beach seemed to be their only hope, if they were to be found by the rescuers who would surely come to look for them. There was nowhere to go in the jungle.

"We can travel along beside the beach," Ling Won said, seeming to have read his thoughts,

69

"and stay under cover of the bushes until we get past those . . . things."

"Right," Chad said. They moved carefully, trying to make no sound, through the screen of vegetation that shielded them from those on the beach.

These were the creatures that shared this planet with them! Chad thought. They looked mean, with those sharp teeth and slimy purple scales—and what would they do with humans if they found them? Probably tear them to pieces and eat them. He walked faster. The singing sounded closer. As Chad tore through a thick bush, he hit his head against a low branch and reeled from the pain of the blow against his already injured forehead. He stepped back involuntarily, and then he saw the creature, a glimmer of purple, hunched against a tree and looking at him. He cried out, and then the three were running in terror, back the way they had come, with Ti-San screaming as though she would never stop.

They ran for what seemed a long time, until finally Ti-San sank to the ground, heaving and shaking, out of breath. Ling Won grabbed her arm. "Come! They might be after us!"

The girl shook her head, and tears glistened on her cheeks. Ling Won grimaced and threw himself to the ground beside her, but Chad stood stiffly against a tree, looking back, straining his ears to hear any sound of pursuit. He could hear only the murmuring of the jungle and the pounding of the surf and the heavy breathing of Ti-San. He relaxed for a moment and closed his eyes, breathing in the sharp, acid smell of the ocean breeze, and then Ti-San cried out. Chad whirled and saw a black, snakelike thing just disappearing into the weeds near the girl's foot, and she was holding her ankle. "It—it stung me!" she cried.

Chad knelt to see. There was a red slash on her ankle, just above her sandal strap. It was deep and wide, and it oozed blood. She moaned with shock and pain.

"Shut up!" her brother told her and bent over the wound. As the two boys watched, the ankle began to swell.

"Do you have a knife?" Chad asked.

71

Ling Won shook his head.

Chad put his mouth to the wound and tried to suck the poison out as Ti-San writhed and cried, but the ankle continued to swell alarmingly. Ling Won took a turn, but finally they could do nothing but stand helplessly, watching Ti-San in her agony.

It was then that they again heard the singing and the sounds of the creatures approaching. The two boys exchanged horrified glances, then quickly moved Ti-San behind the protection of some bushes. Both of them grabbed thick branches from the ground.

The creatures came slowly toward them. There were ten or more—Chad couldn't be sure just how many—and they surrounded the spot where the boys stood. Chad looked at the squat, scaly legs they stood on, the webbed toes, the long forearms that were like tentacles, the pointed snouts, and the round crystal eyes, and he smelled the fishy smell of them. Suddenly he swung his heavy branch at the closest one. The creature fell to the ground, wailing, and the others sang songs of distress as they gathered around it. Then, as two of the creatures picked up the fallen one, the others advanced on the two boys. Chad clutched his branch until his fingers hurt. Ling Won held his over his shoulder, ready to strike. When he heard the sobbing behind him, Chad turned, just in time to see Ti-San stumble out of the bushes on her swollen leg and fall to the ground, unconscious. At the same moment, his arms were pinned behind him.

One of the creatures carried Ti-San. Another pushed Ling Won forward as it held his arms firmly with a slimy tentacle, and Chad was treated in the same way by still another. They were taken down the path they had used once before, toward the top of the hill they had seen, and Chad thought of his family, whom he would probably never see again.

From the hilltop, Chad looked down upon a city of red marble, built against the sides of the cliffs that edged the ocean. No wonder it had never been seen from the aircars that must have flown over it. The cliffs, with their thatch of jungle, overhung the buildings that were the color of the soil, and the city was set in a cove. Some

73

of the structures sat half in and half out of the sea, and Chad could see crowds of the purple creatures moving around them.

Their captors took them into one of the marble buildings. The building seemed to be a series of open balconies, and on either side of it, waterfalls flowed from the cliff top to the ocean. One of the creatures sang to the balconies above them until a net was lowered on a rope of vines. Ti-San was placed in the net, still unconscious, and pulled up. Chad tried to see where they were taking her, but another net was being lowered, and he was being shoved into it along with Ling Won. Then they, too, were moving upward, swinging above the ocean like fish being hauled into a boat, and he could see the creatures below him climbing with ease up the smooth supporting pillars, using only their tentacle forearms.

Chad and Ling Won were taken out of the nets on the top floor, where the side of the cliff rose, steep and bare, behind them, and their captors slithered back down the pillars, singing to each other. The balcony was an empty ledge, damp with the mist from the waterfall close by.

74

Ti-San was not there. Chad threw himself flat on the stone floor, frustrated and exhausted, while Ling Won paced around the balcony, looking down over the waist-high stone balustrades. "There's no way down from here, unless we climb down the pillars," he said.

Chad barely raised his head from his arms, but from this angle he could see Ling Won's injured knee, covered with dried blood and dirt. "How's your leg?" he asked.

Ling Won looked down at it. "Okay, I think. I had forgotten about it. And how is your head?"

Chad grinned. "I seem to have a permanent headache. Otherwise I'm fine." He touched his bandaged forehead gingerly. "At least, we're alive—for the time being."

"Ti-San is alive, too. We will have to find her and take her away."

And then what? Chad thought. They hadn't been able to help her at first, so how could they possibly help her now? He squinted into the white sun. From its position, he guessed it wouldn't set for another four to five hours. Days on this planet were much longer than they were on Earth. There

75

was just that much more time for the scout car to find them—if it was looking for them. He wondered if his father and the two men with him had been taken prisoner, since the boy and girl hadn't been returned to their people. No, it *had* to be that Ling Won's people would realize something had happened to all of them and would join in the search. He stood up and leaned against the balcony railing.

"Look," Chad said to Ling Won, "you're smaller than I am. I could climb over and hold on to the railing here, and you could climb down my body and swing yourself onto the next balcony. That way you might find your sister and maybe even a way to get out of here."

Ling Won looked down. "Perhaps if you climbed down my body instead, you could stand on the railing below, and I could drop to your shoulders. That way both of us could get down."

It was a long, long drop to the ocean below, but there was nothing else they could do, except stay and wait for those creatures to come back. Chad nodded.

Ling Won climbed over the balustrade. The

mist had made it slippery, and Chad saw him lose his balance momentarily. Then he was over the side, wrapping his arms around the stone post that supported the railing, with his legs dangling. Chad went over the railing himself, then grasped Ling Won's shoulders. "Okay?" he grunted into the other's ear.

"Okay." Ling Won's voice was strained.

Chad moved quickly, easing himself down until he was clutching Ling Won's ankles. Trying not to look down, he felt frantically with his feet for the railing below, but his feet touched only emptiness. Ling Won was making anxious sounds above him. Chad looked down. The railing was shining slickly, a long way from his toes. He could never get a foothold on it this way. "I can't reach it," he called up.

Ling Won didn't answer, but Chad felt a sudden jerk and looked up to see him easing his arms from around the post and dropping his body until he was grasping the post with both white-fingered hands.

"Look out!" Chad called.

"Okay. Notches here for a fingerhold. Hurry!"

77

Chad waved his feet furiously, and his toes kicked against the hardness of the railing below him. He laughed with relief. He stood on it carefully, and, as he shouted, "Come on!" he grabbed Ling Won's legs with his hands. The boy's weight came down on Chad's shoulders with a thud, and they both fell forward onto the stone floor. They sat up and grinned at each other.

"One second longer, and we would both have been in the ocean!" Ling Won said, breathing hard.

They looked around, but the balcony, although larger than the one they had been on, was the same. It was empty, and there was no way off it that they could see. Chad looked down over the railing, knowing they would have to do the same thing again and wondering if Ti-San would be on the next balcony. Or would they find only emptiness there, too? And how many balconies could they get to before they fell? He glanced at Ling Won, who stood beside him, looking down, and knew he must be thinking the same thoughts. Right then it seemed very important to Chad that he say one thing. He turned to Ling Won and held out his hand. "We're friends, Ling Won, not enemies."

The other took his hand and pressed it hard. "I think we have always been friends, but we did not know it, because we did not know each other."

Chad nodded. "And so we were afraid. Actually, the war on Earth could have started because some guy was so afraid that he pushed the wrong button."

"And left each country blaming the other," Ling Won said.

Both were silent for a moment, and then Chad said, "We'll have to get down to the next balcony. Can you do it again?"

Before Ling Won could answer, they heard the singing rising to them; then they saw the tentacles and the scaly heads as four of the creatures climbed to the balcony and stood beside them. They sang to each other and to the boys. Then one of them lowered a net he was carrying, and two of them pulled it up again after a few moments.

Ti-San was in the net. She looked at them and

smiled as she was drawn gently over the balustrade, and Chad watched in surprise as the reptile people laid the net carefully on the floor and Ti-San stood up and walked out of it, toward them. Her ankle was bound with red seaweed. "It does not hurt anymore," she told them. "They put some kind of mud on it and bandaged it. Now I am fine."

Ling Won stared at her.

"They are very kind and gentle," Ti-San said. "They sang to me all the time they worked on my ankle. After a while, I forgot the way they looked."

Ling Won smiled suddenly and looked at Chad. "And so all our enemies become our friends," he said.

It took them a while, but through signs and some pictures Chad drew with the contents of one of the food tubes, they made the creatures understand that they wanted to get back to the settlement. Since the beings were amphibians, they had no boats, but after Chad and the others had been lowered from the balcony to the beach below, they demonstrated what a raft looked like, and the creatures set to work, bringing them logs from the jungle and vines to tie them together.

As Ti-San had said, the reptile people were gentle and peaceful. They lived on fish and jungle plants; they played in the sea like otters and sang joyfully to each other on every occasion. Several of them worked on the raft with the boys, and by nightfall, it was finished; but even though the young people were anxious to get back and worried about what their people might be doing to each other because of their absence, they had to wait until dawn. They ate a dinner of sweet, red jungle fruits with the creatures, then lay down on one of the balconies, with occasional sounds of the singing talk and the murmurs of the purple sea lulling them to sleep.

At daybreak, they were accompanied to the raft by a crowd of the strange people, and four of the males helped them push it out into the current. They waved good-bye to those on the shore, but the four who had helped them swam along beside the raft, guiding it and pushing it,

81

sometimes resting on it for a while and then sliding back into the water again to pilot it through the waves.

"They apparently want to come with us," Chad said to Ling Won as they watched the shining, scaly bodies undulating in the water beside them. "I'd be glad if my dad and the others could meet them."

"Are you not forgetting what they look like?" Ling Won reminded him. "They will be mistaken for monsters."

"Not when we tell everybody what they did for us."

The creatures guided the raft along the coast, and while Chad and Ling Won scanned the beaches for any sign of human beings, Ti-San sat at the edge of the raft and practiced singing the same notes the purple creatures were singing. This seemed to amuse them, and they laughed and gave her longer phrases to imitate.

"You had better be careful," Ling Won told her. "They might be teaching you bad words in their language." But Ti-San told him he was only jealous because he couldn't carry a tune.

The journey was fun, but Chad was relieved when they finally spotted two men fishing off a rocky point. At last he would find out if his father and the others were safe. The three young people called and waved. It wasn't until the raft was pushed nearer the shore that Chad saw the men were Ling Won's people, not his own, but that was all right.

The four reptile people flipped out of the water and stood on the raft with them, singing eagerly and pointing to the men with their tentacles. But the men were running away now, and when the raft was close enough to the beach for all of them to jump into the water and run to shore, there was nobody in sight.

"The creatures scared them," Ling Won said as they started across the beach.

There was a sudden shriek from Ti-San, behind them, and the two boys whirled just in time to see a large red rock beside one of the reptile men disintegrate in a flash of light. Then Chad saw the crowd gathering among the trees, just beyond the beach, the men with their L-guns aimed at them.

84

Ti-San and Ling Won saw them, too, and cried out anguished words in their own language, until finally the men lowered their guns and stood warily waiting for them. The reptile people fluttered their tentacles helplessly and made anxious sounds, but Ti-San spoke to them with a soothing voice, coaxing them to accompany her. Chad waited while she and Ling Won embraced their father and mother and explained the presence of the purple creatures, but even after their explanation, everyone seemed to be frightened of them and refused to go near them.

Chad finally got a chance to talk to Ling Won's father. "Is my dad all right?"

The man looked at him with cold eyes. "You and your people tried to kidnap my children. Your father and his friends have been held hostage for their safe return. Now that they are back, we shall see."

"Father, we were *not* kidnapped," Ling Won said impatiently.

Chad felt a pang of fear. "What did you do to them? Where are they?"

The man turned silently and led the way

through the trees. The crowd followed, whispering and pointing at the strange creatures, who walked with their three friends.

"What would your people do with my dad and the others?" Chad asked Ling Won anxiously.

The boy shook his head. "You will see them in a few minutes. I am sure they have not been harmed."

Then they came to the place where the silver ship stood, and Chad saw his father and the other two men. Each was tied with a rope to a tree near the ship, the rope fastened in such a way around his neck and arms that he had to crouch to keep from strangling. The three were obviously in agony. Chad raced to them, calling, and his father raised his head wearily, watching him through heavy-lidded eyes. When he realized that it was really Chad running toward him, Lan Reynolds managed a smile.

"Dad! What have they done to you?" Chad tugged at the knots frantically as Ling Won and his father approached.

"I'm all right," Chad's father said weakly. "Thank God you're all back safe. We were afraid of what might have happened to you."

"We're in a lot better shape than the three of you," Chad said as Ling Won's father began cutting the ropes with a long knife.

"I offer my apologies," Ling Won's father said coolly. "My children have explained what happened. If you had been in my place, you would have done the same."

The three prisoners were freed, and they moved about unsteadily for a few minutes, stretching their cramped muscles. While Chad told them his story, Ti-San, looking heartbroken, brought them food and drink from the ship, and Ling Won's father brought back the L-guns that had been taken away from them. He seemed defensive rather than really sorry, Chad thought, and his group and Lan Reynolds's group spoke to each other with cold correctness.

"We'll have to get back to the settlement as soon as possible," Chad's father told him when he had eaten. "They know we're here, and I'm sure that by now they're planning an attack to free us."

Ling Won shook his head. "Wars and hatred

87

and suffering," he said. "They do not stop, even on this planet." Chad nodded, looking sadly at his father and his two friends as they sat on the ground, eating, and then at Ling Won's father, who sat with a group of men nearby, watching.

A short distance away, the four purple creatures were examining the spaceship, singing excitedly as Ti-San showed it to them. She turned, smiling, and ran toward her father, crying, "Can I show them inside?" and then her weakened ankle gave way, and she fell. In a moment, the four reptile people were hurrying to help her, singing sharp notes of distress, and the men were all on their feet, their L-guns drawn.

Chad shouted, "They won't hurt her!" but it was too late. As one of the creatures reached toward the girl, one of his shining tentacles disintegrated. He fell with a shriek, and the others drew back.

There was a moment of awful silence, and then Ti-San slowly got up and knelt by the injured creature. She cradled his scaly head in her lap and sobbed. Ling Won and Chad both got between the humans and the creatures, and
88

Chad, too, found himself crying with rage and shame. "Stop it! Stop it, all of you!" he shouted. "How many lives have to be destroyed before you realize? *You* are the ones who kill. You kill what you fear—and you fear anything you don't understand!"

His own people and Ling Won's people all stared at him. Finally one man said, "But those beasts were going to harm the girl!"

"Those beasts saved our lives and brought us home!" Chad was almost screaming now.

Ling Won spoke more quietly, but Chad heard the disgust in his voice. "We found friendship with each other—and with those 'creatures'—in the short time we were away. To find enemies, we had to return to our own people!"

It seemed to Chad then that their words might have been understood. Hesitantly, the men put their guns away and some of them went to offer medical aid to the reptile man. His three companions were carrying him away, but even now, still instinctively trusting and friendly, they agreed to take him into the ship instead.

"They're gentle, innocent people," Chad told

his father as they stood beside Ling Won and his father. "Life on this planet could be peaceful."

Lan Reynolds nodded. "We were searching for peace when we came here. Maybe you're right. Maybe we can find it only when we forget the old fears and suspicions." He turned to the man who had been his enemy and held out his hand, and, after a moment, the other man smiled and took it.

BUCK
AND
THE
GENTS
FROM
SPACE

by Mack Reynolds

WHEN THE FIRST SHIP FROM SPACE landed on
Earth, it never landed on no White House lawn,
nor on that there Red Square in Moscow. It
landed right smack on Sam Dillard's spread, just
a mite north of Sage City, New Mexico, maybe
half a day's ride in a jeep or a pickup truck. Fact
is, so did the second one and the third one, but
that part of it comes later, when Buck started
interplanetary peace. That first time, though, he
nigh on to ended it!

Well, sir, what happened was this. Buck was

doin' some chores round the ranch house. His paw and Chavez, the hired hand, was off fixin' some fence over to Arroyo Seco. They'd maybe be back about dark, and he was cookin' up his lunch and their supper. Mostly Buck did the cookin' since Chavez's wife run off back to Mexico—couldn't stand it livin' on the ranch and bein' purely lonely, there not bein' any other womenfolk. He'd learned most of his cookin' from *Señora* Chavez. Ain't much to learn about ranch and Mexican cookin', but he liked to do it the best he could.

Anyways, it all kinda started when this here contraption—looked somethin' like a big flyin' saucer—comes landin' down in the backyard, over near to the chicken coop.

Now, it wasn't like as if Buck'd never seed a flyin' saucer before. In fact, he and his paw didn't know where the flyin' saucers left off and these here new government folderols begun. The Dillard spread seemed to be located at some sorta crossroads, like. These things'd go whizzin' by, sometimes at night and sometimes durin' the day, and they was the most confounded-lookin' things

ever: jets and rockets and flyin' wings and saucers and whatever not. After a spell, Buck and
his paw didn't hardly bother to look up. His paw
told him to keep his tater trap shut about 'em in
town, or folks'd start callin' 'em loco.

Anyways, Buck put down the two pails he was
carryin' to the pigpen and moseyed over to see
if they'd maybe had a forced landin' or somethin'.

It was when the first one come out of this
round door in the side that Buck kinda gulped
and said, "Holy hominy!"

Seems as if this here stranger was a kinda fun
ny red color and looked some like the Pinheaded
Man from Yucatan they had in the freak show
when the carnival come to Sage City last year.
He was all done up in a spankin' new uniform,
though, and he looked around him real sharp,
not like no pinhead.

He seen nobody is around but Buck, so he
calls somethin' back over his shoulder, and out
of the flyin' saucer comes two green-faced gents.
Guess it was stretchin' to call 'em gents—not
human-type gents, at least. Later on, Buck
wouldn't even try to describe 'em; says nobody

93

would believe him, anyhow.

Well, out in the desert, ever'body's got to be downright hospitable, if anybody's goin' to get along at all. So Buck says, "Howdy, strangers, come in and set awhile."

The first stranger looks around kinda nasty, and with a voice somethin' like a rusty tin can, he says, "From the radio emanations from which we deciphered your language, one would never expect your planet to look like this."

Buck, he'd always been kinda proud of his old man's spread, realizin' that someday, when he'd growed up, he'd be takin' it over. Course, the ranch was a mite dry—take maybe ten or twenty acres to graze a steer—but they had a good view over Dead Man's Gulch, and Furnace Rock ain't no more'n five miles away, where the wagon train got no further and nigh on to two hundred folks died of thirst, more'n a century ago.

So Buck says, modest-like, "It *is* kinda prettier around here than most places."

One of the other strangers says to the first one, "We must assume this vicinity to be one of their most advanced. Much of the atomic radiation is from the immediately surrounding area."

That didn't surprise Buck none, Los Alamos bein' only maybe fifty miles away, but he wasn't gettin' the drift of what these gents wanted.

They kinda looked him over for a minute, Buck standin' there in the cutdown levis his paw had passed on to him and with that battered old low-crown hat of his settin' on the back of his head and him barefooted, and they kinda shake their heads like, but finally the first one says, "I am Demy Tass, Third Garoon of Mars, and these are my loyal followers and colleagues, Fren Fries, High Nork of Venus, and Mil Toas, First Chef, Jupiterian Satellite Confederation."

Well, Buck, he ain't never heard tell of their towns, but he could see they was foreigners and they prob'ly couldn't help the way they looked. Anyways, he just said, "Howdy, gents. I'm Buck Dillard, Box One-O-Four, Rural Route Three, Sage City, New Mexico."

"An imposing title," says Demy Tass. "Perhaps we were mistaken and have misjudged your rank."

It only comes to Buck then that these here

strangers figured he was a grown-up. It was only a mite surprisin', on account of Buck was middlin' big for his age, and they was kinda small for theirn. In fact, Buck had an inch or two on all three of 'em. He didn't tell 'em contrariwise, on account of it kinda set him up a mite to be taken for a full-grown *hombre*.

Well, Buck, he takes 'em inside and sets 'em down in the parlor, where him and his paw and Chavez never go unless womenfolk or the preacher comes visitin'. And then he goes on out to the kitchen and gets Chavez's jug of tequila. Buck's paw didn't hold with drinkin' likker, but Chavez used to like a nip of the Mexican red-eye once in a while, and he kept it in the kitchen cupboard. Buck gets three big jelly glasses and pours a glassful for each one and sets the jug on the table, handy for any that might want another.

"This is the real stuff," he tells them. "Chavez, the hired man, he brings it up from Mexico. Says it packs a real wallop."

I guess good manners is more or less the same ever'wheres. At any rate, these three strangers, they up with their glasses and stiff-wrist their tequila down, and then they kinda discover they made a big mistake. Them that had the green faces turned red, while the one that had the red face turned white. Then they got to their feet and pranced around a mite, somethin' like the Apache Snake Dance, only, of course, they didn't have no snakes in their mouths. Maybe they woulda preferred a snake, at that.

Finally they stop, still breathin' kinda hard, and this leadin' one, Demy Tass, he whips a long gadget out'n his belt—looks somethin' like a flashlight with a pistol handle—and points it at Buck. But the other two, they start talkin' to him in some foreign gibberish, and by and by he puts his flashlight, or whatever it was, back into his belt and kinda glares at Buck.

Well, Buck, he could see there'd been some kinda mix-up come and gone, so he indicates the jug of tequila and says, "Help yourself, gents. Holy hominy, Chavez says that's the best drinkin' likker in the country!"

"You mean"—the leader pointed at the jug—"that is the national beverage? Your people drink that *on purpose?*" All three seemed impressed.

97

Then he kinda shook his head and says, "We shall get to the affair at hand, having no time to investigate your quaint folk customs, such as giving strangers things like that to drink. However, if cultural domination of Mars is proven, which I am sure it will be, I shall do my best to eliminate this practice that can only be a remnant of barbarism."

Well, Buck, he didn't get much of that, but he tried to look polite. He figures they're lost and was probably heading for Albuquerque or Santa Fe. When it gets cleared up just what they got in mind, he can maybe saddle up old Flapjack, ride over to the Perkins Ranch, and phone from there to whoever they was supposed to get in touch with.

Demy Tass gets to the point, like he said. "It is not until a planet reaches a high degree of scientific and cultural development that we reveal the existence of the Solar System League," says he. "When such development is attained, the new planet, or satellite, is, ah, *invited* to join the League."

Buck was just a youngster, of course, but he

was sharp like a tack, and he noticed when this gent said "invited," he had a kinda silky tone to his voice. But Buck couldn't follow too good what he was sayin', anyways, so he didn't make much mind.

"The degree of scientific development needed is the use of nuclear fission," Demy Tass says, "but that is the less important. Cultural attainments are the basis of our social system, the foundations of our society. He who dominates culturally"—his voice gets kinda high and inspired-like, and he raises his right hand kinda like to strengthen his point—"dominates economically and governmentally."

"I reckon I get that," Buck says. "You mean like music and paintin' and such folderol. That's what counts with you folks."

"Bah!" says Fren Fries, the one from Venus.

"Not at all!" says Demy Tass, kinda horrified-like. "Long millenia ago, such secondary arts were passed by. The arts of the eye, the arts of the ear, are nothing to the—"

"The art of the palate!" chimes in the one named Mil Toas.

99

"Yes," says Demy Tass, dramatic-like again. "The supreme art of them all! The art of the palate—the sense of taste."

"You mean you folks like your grub, huh?" says Buck, still tryin' to put over that he's as grown-up as they are. "Well, sir, you met a real *compañero* here, gents." He adds, modest-like, "There's folks around here say I'm as good a campfire cook as you'll find this side of Denver."

Actual, it wasn't too much of a brag. Buck's paw was mighty proud of how much cookin' Buck had picked up from *Señora* Chavez, who'd once run a chili house in Laredo.

This sets Demy Tass back a mite. "You mean," says he, "you are an artist of cuisine? You are a gourmet and a gourmand of reputation?"

In spite of these here foreign words they're always usin', Buck gets their drift. He says, still modest, "My boiled puddin' is the best in three counties. I hope you won't spread it around, but the secret is stickin' in a good handful of cactus apples."

Well, sir, you can see they're all impressed by this, seein' as they all come to their feet and make a kind of a short bow to Buck. Just to be polite, he stands, too, and bows back, and then ever'body sets down again and Demy Tass goes on.

"As I say, it is cultural development that prevails in the Solar System League. Each decade, a great conclave is held, and the outstanding artists of each member planet compete. That planet which prevails rules, governmentally and economically, until the next conclave."

He looks kind of modest hisself and says, "In the last conclave, we of Mars dominated with my Martian iguana *à la crème.*"

"With Callisto truffles," Fren Fries adds, sadlike but admirin'.

"Although," says Mil Toas, kinda sharp, "My Io eel *en papillote* had the judges in a quandary for long hours, so close did it come."

Buck said, "To tell you the truth, gents, I was just gettin' my lunch cooked up, back in the kitchen, when you come down. It bein' a long time since I whipped up some *chiles rellenos,* I just went to the bother. Mexican stuffed peppers. I'd be proud to have you set down with me for

101

grub. Nobody else on this here spread'll be back till night."

Well, sir, Demy Tass, he looks at the other two and they look at him, and the three of 'em seem to come to some sorta agreement, although they don't have to talk. You can see their faces kinda square up, serious-like, and their shoulders straighten, and they come to their feet and bow, real stiff, to Buck; so he stands, too, and bows back, then leads 'em into the big ranch house kitchen, where he and his paw and Chavez always eat.

He sets 'em down at the table, shoves plates around, and is about to go for knives and forks, when he notices each of 'em just opens a fancy pouch at their belt and outs with tools of their own that look like they might be made outa solid gold.

Well, Buck, he goes over to the stove and finishes up the *chiles rellenos* and heats up some *tortillas*. He's got some *frijoles,* left over from the day before, on the back of the stove, and he figures he can stretch out the stuffed hot peppers with 'em.

102

The three strangers, they kinda pretend they ain't watchin' him, but he can see from the side of his eyes they take their grub serious, all right, because each one is actual watchin' him real close, to see if they can pick up any secrets he might let drop.

Buck, he plunks the grub down on the table and then sets to, ranch style, without no preliminary folderol. He slips about a pint of *frijoles* onto his plate, piles four or five chilies on top, grabs up a *tortilla,* and says, "Fall to, gents; eat hearty," just like he was his paw with invited guests.

He takes up half a chili and puts it in his mouth. While he's chewin' it, he says, "Holy hominy, gents, in this country, this is what we call real grub." He had heard his paw say that, too.

Well, sir, you can see they're impressed. One by one, they load up their plates, the same way Buck had hisn. And then, all three together, they each stuff half a *chile relleno* into their face and begin to chew.

Buck looks up at 'em to see how they're

103

enjoyin' his cookin', and he kinda sees this look come over their faces. In no time at all, it must've occurred to 'em that they didn't exact want this in their mouths. Them that had the green faces turned red, and the one had the red face, he turns white, and then they got up on their feet and begun to prance around a mite, the way they had before—hard to describe, unless you ever seen the Apache Snake Dance.

Then they made a beeline for the water pump —must've known instinctive-like what it was— and they begun pumpin' so fast the handle was a blur.

Well, Buck, he just sets there and kinda stares at 'em, and they're whooshin' and breathin' hard and gulpin' down water and fannin' their mouths with their hands, and all this goes on maybe five, ten minutes.

By and by, they face Buck again, and this Demy Tass, he hauls out with his flashlight thing, but the other two argue with him, and by and by he puts it away, reluctant.

They just give Buck one more look woulda made the scales fall off'n a rattlesnake, and they turn around on their heels and march back to their saucer ship. They climb into it, and in no time at all, they're outa sight.

It weren't till some time later that Buck, he got to rememberin' some of them space TV shows he seen over at the Perkins Ranch and kinda wondered if them three gents was just foreigners—or really *foreigners*. Whatever, they sure didn't like chili peppers.

When his paw and Chavez come back to the ranch house that night, all tuckered out, Buck's paw says, kinda sour, "What's all that mess over nearby the chicken coop? Looks like somethin's been burnin' there."

The last time Buck had told his paw a whopper, he'd got took back to the woodshed for a good hidin'. And, like I say, he's sharp as a tack, for his age.

So he says, "What mess, paw? I didn't see no mess."

Chavez takes his jug of tequila and swishes it around, kinda checkin' like how much was left. Then he kinda scowls and looks over at Buck. But then he shakes his head. He knows, darn tootin' well, no thirteen-year-old is gonna be gettin' into his red-eye. Stuff'd take the enamel right off'n your teeth.

Well, sir, that was how Buck come up against the first flyin' saucer and how he nigh on to got this here world into a space war. The next time, they was two of 'em, and that's the time he *settled* a space war.

What happened was, Buck was out after a few cottontails he figured he'd fry for his paw and Chavez. He'd saddled up old Flapjack and fetched his .22 and headed up to Lake Hill, up into the mountains a piece from the spread. It was maybe two or three months since he'd had the run-in with the three gents who liked their grub but not hisn.

Now, your best way to hunt rabbits with a shotgun is to walk along slow and scare 'em up and hit 'em on the run. But if all you got is a .22, it ain't so easy. So Buck, he had hisself a system. He sat hisself down real quiet 'mong the trees, and he just waited. They was a lot of cottontails around about there, and he knew by and by he'd spot one settin' down, and *bang!* he'd have it. Buck was a pretty good shot, and his paw had give him this here little gun 'bout two years ago. Most kids in the West git their first gun 'bout that age.

But Buck's not settin' there in the woods more'n maybe five minutes, when he sees a glint like the sun reflectin' on somethin' way up above, and he thinks maybe one of the passenger planes comin' down from Denver way might be passin'. But it ain't. The glint gits brighter, and Buck looks up, and *whoosssh!* somethin' comes sweepin' down and lands in a little clearin' not more'n twenty, thirty feet from where Buck is settin' real quiet, waitin' for some of the rabbits to show up.

Buck says later he recalls the thing bein' kinda round, like a short cigar, but it moves so fast and blurry that he can't rightly remember too good.

No sooner does it come to rest here in this clearin' than a door—kinda triangle-like, Buck says it was, not like a door you'd have in a house —opens up, and out comes, fast as he can move, a little gent'd go maybe three and a half feet tall and kinda purple-faced. He rolls hisself, tail over

107

elbow, away from the little ship, out of the clearin', and into a kinda depression already half-full of springwater. Winds up not more'n a few yards from Buck.

Just in time, too, 'cause Buck sees another glint from up above, and there's another *whoosssh,* and a bright light comes down, like you'd think it was the beam of a big flashlight if it was nighttime, but this was bright right in the midst of day. The light kinda touches the little purple gent's ship, and it starts smokin' and meltin' away, and, before you could tell, it was gone—without one sign of where it'd been.

Course, all this only took a couple of seconds or so, and Buck was kinda settin' there gawkin' at these goin's-on. Here he was, just waitin' for a rabbit to hop along. But, like I keep sayin', Buck's sharp for his age, and he figures it's a off day for rabbits, and he just goes on settin' there. He's tied up Flapjack some ways away, so he don't have to worry none about him.

No sooner was this here first little ship melted away and gone than *whoosssh!* down comes a second one, almost like to the first, only different
108

a slight. Comes down and lands in the same clearin' Buck is on the edge of and the little purple *hombre* is in the ditch near to, and another queer-lookin' little gent, about the same size as the first one but maybe almost twice as fat, comes out. Buck says this one looks somethin' like a tourist from New York, only his face is colored orange.

Now, since thinkin' over the first three gents and the TV shows over to the Perkins Ranch, Buck has decided these two are from some other planet. They just plain can't be from no place on this world.

No sooner is the second one out'n his space boat and kinda peerin' around, satisfied with hisself like, than this little purple one hidin' in the hole near Buck ups with a funny-lookin' gadget, somethin' like a section of rubber hose, and squirts a beam at the second one.

Down goes the orange one fast, just in time, and he rolls hisself out of the way and into the bed of a little stream. Lucky for him it's been a kinda dry summer, and there ain't no water in it.

Well, sir, it must've been a shock to the orange

110

one to find out the purple gent was still up and around and ready to continue the feud, whatever its cause mighta been. But he tugs out a gadget of his own—looks somethin' like a eggbeater to Buck, but he never did get a very good look at it—and fires away with a kinda boilin' brown light that just misses the purple one by inches and knocks half a dozen branches off'n a mesquite tree.

Buck sees the kinda beams and rays these gents is cuttin' off at each other with and figures, if they don't look out, they'll set a fire that'd never git put out, it bein' so far away and all from a good road. The rangers'd have their work cut out just gittin' to it. Besides, Buck is just about 'twixt the two of 'em, and he don't know how long it might be before one or t'other of 'em misses and hits him.

Now, up to this here time, neither of the two critters had spotted Buck, they was so wrapped up in each other and so excited, and here Buck was, no more'n a few yards away from the little purple one.

Before he had time to think it out just what he

111

was doin', he takes two or three long steps and reaches out and picks up this here purple one and swoops him up under his arm; didn't weigh no more'n maybe twenty-five pounds. Then Buck starts for the second one, shakin' his .22 and hollerin' if they didn't cut out all this tally-hootin' around, he'd give 'em what for.

Well, sir, you can imagine how surprised the two of 'em was. Here the purple one finds hisself ketched up under Buck's arm, and the orange one, he sees Buck comin' at him all of a sudden —hadn't even seed him before—wavin' his rifle and totin' the purple one under his arm.

Before the orange one could up with his eggbeater gadget, Buck was to him and standin' right in front of him, madder'n a Gila monster and hollerin' for him to cut out all this here folderol, before they set fire to the woods.

The orange one just stands there, kinda blinkin', lookin' at the purple one tucked under Buck's arm and kickin' and yellin' in a shrill little voice, like he was fit to be tied.

So Buck puts the little *hombre* down on the ground and kinda brushes him off a mite. He has

112

a nice little uniform on, but 'twixt the water in that hole and all the dirt and leaves and ever'-thin', he sure looked a mess now.

Both of 'em is speechless at the way this is turned out, them not expectin' it, but Buck says, kinda mild now, "What're you two up to, any-ways? Got no more sense than to go chompin' and howlin' around like that?"

The orange one kinda glares at Buck and says, "If it hadn't been for your interference, this ene-my of the chosen would have gone to join his misbegotten ancestors."

T'other one says somethin' that sounds like "Hah!" and his hand starts comin' up again with his gadget, but Buck scowls at him real hard, so he puts it back in his belt.

Buck says, "All right, now, supposin' we just set down and figure this here out. Can't have you two *hombres* settin' fire to the woods and cuttin' the trees down and all."

Well, sir, they're still kinda dazed by Buck poppin' up and gittin' 'em into a spot where they can't rightly use their gadgets on each other, so they kinda simmer down, at least to where they

113

just glare at each other whilst they answer Buck's questions.

Buck says, "First of all, how come you gents talk American? Ain't hard to see you're from elsewheres."

"Radio emanations," snaps the purple one, not takin' his eyes from the orange feller. "We, the chosen race of Deneb, find it necessary at times to communicate with the Aldebaran vermin. Rather than speak their degenerate tongue or allow them to speak our lordly language, we compromise and use the language of Earth."

"I'll be doggoned," Buck says. Looked to him like just about ever'body and his cousin was learnin' to talk American from listenin' to the radio broadcasts.

The orange one was mad as a boiled billy owl at what the other *hombre* said. "The opposite is true," he snaps out. "We Aldebarans would not descend to speaking the foul language of Deneb, nor would we allow them to learn our sacred tongue. Hence we have compromised and learned your most prevalent Earth language."

"Comes to 'bout the same thing," Buck murmurs. He was feelin' awful growed-up, talkin' to these two fellers, maybe 'cause he was so much bigger than them. He says, "Let's get to the point. Just what're you two gents doin' all this here scrappin' about? Here you come hundreds of miles, maybe more, from your own places, and what'd you do? 'Stead of goin' fishin' together —Lake Hill's got some of the best fishin' for mountain trout in the state—you start bangin' away like a coupla locos."

First they looked at him like he'd plumb lost his marbles and didn't make no sense at all. The purple one, kinda dignified-like, says, "Denebians and Aldebarans have been engaged in internecine warfare for millennia. While you comparatively backward earthlings were still building pyramids on the Nile River, our every effort was already directed against each other."

Buck could see, right then and there, this was one awful feud goin' on 'twixt these purple folks and orange folks. He hadn't never heerd tell of no Nile River, but that wasn't important.

Buck says, "Let's talk this out a mite, gents. What're you warrin' for? With all them there

115

gadgets and beams and all, you must cut each other up somethin' awful."

Well, with that, they both started accusin' each other of startin' the big trouble, but it comes out, in no time at all, that it all happened so far back, neither rightly knew just what did happen.

So Buck says, kinda soothin'-like, since he didn't want 'em rarin' off again, burnin' up the woods, "Seems to me you all'd be better off if you tried bein' more neighborly."

That started 'em off again, and Buck noticed they'd lost any antagonism they mighta had against him and was just hollerin' 'twixt theirselves. So he says, "Holy hominy, ain't you never figured out you oughta do to the other gent the way you'd like him to do to you?"

Well, sir, you'd never believe it, but that kinda stopped 'em, and Buck could see both of 'em was thinking it out.

The orange one kinda looks at him and says, "Earthling, that is a beautiful thought." You can see he's plenty set back.

The purple one nods to that and is kinda frownin'. He kinda mumbles, "If everyone fol-

lowed such a philosophy. . . ." But then he shakes
his head and scowls at the orange one. "Possibly
the chosen of Deneb are capable of assimilating
such a lofty ethic, but we must defend ourselves
against the vermin of Aldebaran."

That started the little orange *hombre* off again,
but Buck hushed 'em both.

He said, "If folks ain't been gittin' along, it's
the one that starts bein' nice to t'other first that's
goin' to feel best about patchin' it up."

He settles hisself down on the stump, feelin'
pretty set-up for a young feller, seein' as how
these two gents from space was listenin' to him
just like he was full-growed. He says, "Now, supposin' one of you come up to me and whomped
me one on the face. Supposin', 'stead of whomp-
in' you back, I just naturally changed my face
about so as to give you another chance. Now,
how'd you feel about that?"

Well, that set 'em back again. You could see
them little *hombres,* no matter what size or color
they might be, was ready thinkers.

Buck says, "Now, here's the same idea, only
put a different way." He notices the orange one
117

took a little pad and is notin' down, in a funny scribblin' writin', what Buck says. "It's purely better to give somebody else somethin' nice than it is to git somethin' yourself. It makes you feel better inside."

Well, sir, you'd never believe how quick those two little gents took to what Buck was tellin' 'em. No time at all, there they was, settin' side by side, listenin' to him. And pretty soon the orange one is apologizin' to the purple one for burnin' up his spaceship, and the purple one says not to make nothin' of it, 'cause it was gittin' old and rusty, anyways, and it was practically a favor, what with it bein' insured and all.

Buck says, "If you gents listen to our radio, how come you ain't already heard these ideas? Most every mornin', specially Sundays, you can tune in on these here ideas."

But the purple one, he says, "Holy One, we of the other worlds had no idea your teachings could be heard on radio. The times we attempted to tune in daytime broadcasts we—" he kinda shuddered—"were unfortunate enough to receive, ah, soap operas, I believe they are called. To

118

avoid them, we have listened only to programs from five on, many of them news broadcasts. And I assure you, Holy One, there is nothing in them to suggest that your fellow earthlings have ever heard of your teachings."

Finally Buck figures he better git on back to the ranch house to fix supper for his paw and Chavez, so he stands up and says, "Well, I have to be gittin' along. You two gents oughta go back where you come from and tell your folks what I said. Ain't no sense at all in feudin' away like you do."

By this time, they was both kinda hangin' their heads, and the both of 'em was takin' down notes, each in his own handwritin', and every time they looked up at Buck, their eyes were kinda shiny-like.

So the orange one says, "Holy One, do you mean that you commission us to return to our respective worlds and spread your word?"

Buck thinks about that, feelin' pretty important-like, and says, "Why, sure. More folks git to hearin' the way they should act, better it'll be."

"We hear and we obey," says the purple one,

119

and the orange one allows all the people on Aldebaran is ready to hear tell of such ideas, and they'll spread over the planet like a brush fire, and the purple one, he allows Deneb is the same way.

So the two of 'em, kinda bowin' their heads, back away from Buck to the one remainin' spaceship, and they climb into it, friendly to each other as can be, and off they go, *whoossh!*

Buck kinda looks after 'em for a mite and says out loud, "Shucks, I wonder if them little *hombres* got the idea them teachin's was mine original. Seems as if they ain't got no Sunday schools where they come from."

Well, he goes and gits Flapjack and rides on back to the ranch house, and his paw and Chavez are settin' at the kitchen table playin' checkers, the day's chores bein' all done.

They both see that Buck don't have no rabbits, and they grin, but they don't say nothin'.

Buck starts puttin' supper together, and finally he says, kinda thoughtful-like, "Sometimes I wonder if we got any right to go off into the woods and shoot them little cottontails. Maybe

120

they got just as much right to live as us."

Well, that sets his paw off to laughin', not knowin' the real reason Buck come back without no rabbits. He figures that Buck is purely tryin' to find some excuse for his bad luck.

He says, "Buck Dillard, the natural-born revival preacher and vegetarian." And he turns to Chavez, who's grinnin' wide. "Can you imagine this youngster of mine ever growin' up to be a evangelist?"

"Oh, I don't know," says Buck.

A MATTER OF CHOICE

by B. J. Lytle

WE MARCHED BRISKLY across the schoolyard in three long rows, each row composed of twenty-five boys. We were uniformly dressed in white coveralls. Each head was blond; the top of each head was exactly four feet five inches from the ground. We marched with military precision, taking our daily quota of exercise.

I knew that each head was filled with the same thoughts: the equations given us in our last class, by a computer—each head but one, that is.

I couldn't have cared less about the equations.

122

I was thinking treasonous thoughts, thinking of home and my parents.

Not that home was any better than it was here at school. At home my parents lived in a two-room co-op, all that we were allowed in a vastly overpopulated world. The street where we lived was lined with matching co-ops. One had to watch the house numbers carefully to avoid going into the wrong building, something that had happened to me more than once in my eleven years. Also, at home, when I wanted to play outdoors, I had to walk six blocks to a small park, where I had to stand in line if I wanted to swing or slide or get a drink from the fountain or do anything at all.

It was a little better at school. The boys were never allowed on the playground all at the same time. We came in staggered groups, thus keeping the grounds full of boys at all times but avoiding overcrowding as much as possible.

I lived and slept in a room with twenty-five other boys, but each of us had his own bed and his own chest in which to store personal treasures, and there were curtains we could draw to

123

allow a certain amount of privacy.

Yes, school was really all right. I had no complaints, except for the fact that I had to study science. When my parents were granted permission to have a child, the Supreme Command studied the future needs of the world and decided that scientists would be most in demand. My parents underwent extensive examinations, and when it was ascertained that they could produce a scientist, they were allowed to have me. Scientific knowledge was programmed into me before birth. Somehow, the system made a mistake with me, and the plain fact was that I didn't want to be a scientist.

I tried being friends with some of my fellow students. I was reasonably cheerful and should have made friends easily, but when I was truthful and told them my real feelings, they withdrew from me, thinking me radical. Perhaps I was. It was unheard of for a boy to change his field of study or to resent following orders. They treated me like some kind of defective, and I soon learned to keep quiet and pretend interest in the things they were interested in.

As a result, I was uptight and unhappy. When the government medical officers gave us our regular examinations, I said nothing, but they noticed the tenseness and the attitude of indifference. They decided that I needed more vitamins, so now I had excess energy coursing through my body and no outlet for it.

My parents were unusual people. Both worked in the social planning sector and were expert at their jobs. But at home, at night, they talked of very different things. They were both well educated; they knew their history and how the world had been in the last century—free, with open country, trees and grass, and families living in single houses, before overcrowding became so bad. They knew also that their ancestors had been free to work at the jobs of their choice, not on orders from the government.

Back then, people didn't look so much alike, either, as they did now, due to the perfected, nonrisk method of reproduction. Best of all, in the past, things grew in the world—plants, trees, flowers, and food. Now the food was manufactured, condensed, containing the vitamins and

125

minerals needed, but not resembling the old-style food in any way.

My parents were dissatisfied with their world, and some of their talk, naturally, I overheard. I shared their opinions. I once heard my father say that perhaps it would have been better if the bomb his ancestors had feared so much had exploded. At least it would have taken care of the overpopulation. Of course, he didn't really mean that. Something should have been done, though, he said. The human race had grown too fast, had defiled the rivers, the land, and the air, had killed off the animals, had been filled with greed. The result was this temperature-controlled, domed, crowded world in which a man no longer had any choice or any control over his own destiny.

These hefty thoughts were what filled my head as I marched with my fellow students. Somehow, I told myself, I would do something. I wouldn't grow up following the masses, with complete mindlessness, content only to do my job and obey orders. I wanted more than that. I would be a pioneer.

That night, after lights-out, when all the other

boys were asleep, I lay awake, thinking. I had a
germ of an idea, based on something I had overheard my father talking about: a newly discovered planet that they had named New America,
hoping for the rich promise of that original country and planning to use experience in making it
better this time. The environment was much the
same as Earth's. There was light and room and
air. Plant and animal life had evolved, but not
human life. A handful of colonists were already
established there—a select few—but to become
a colonist, one had to be found worthy. In a
world filled with so many billions of people, the
competition was terrific. Mere willingness to go
counted for very little.

I tossed in my bed, wishing for sleep but unable to stop the workings of my rebellious mind.
At last I told myself that it was no use, and, holding that thought, I fell asleep.

In the next few weeks, I was unable to keep
my mind on my studies. For the first time, my
grades went below the accepted level, and stern-
er measures were called for—in my case, an
order to appear before the school director.

I was trembling when I knocked at the director's office door, and I felt as if my legs couldn't carry me as I approached the large desk, behind which the stern, white-haired man sat.

"Sit down, Steven Greenleaf," the director said.

I sat down. In the massive armchair, I felt myself shrink into insignificance. No longer did I feel like a young man, almost grown. I felt like the youngest, smallest kindergartener.

"What has happened to you, Steven?" the director asked, somewhat less sternly. "Your grades— We know you have the intelligence, the potential, to do better. We have all your records. We *know*."

Yes, I thought. *They know. They know everything. There are no secrets, no feelings that they are not aware of. Their charts unveil my whole life. I might as well tell him.*

I did tell him. I poured out all of my rebellious thoughts, all my secret cravings, my longing to be free, my need to work in the soil and grow things and help to found a new world, like the old one but built with much more wisdom. Once

I started talking, I found it easy. I was a goner, anyway, I decided. For a boy to rebel against the school system was unheard of. I had no idea what would happen to me. There were no similar cases, at least to my knowledge. I suspected that they would institutionalize me, marking me as a misfit unable to function any longer in the world. Well, I told myself, I didn't care. I would rather be shut away than to live as I was told to live.

During my outpouring, the director sat silent, no expression at all on his face, certainly no trace of surprise. Maybe he *has* heard all this before, I thought, but from whom?

He gave me permission to leave his office, and my next few weeks were filled with dread. I felt something ominous hanging over me, and I wished with all my being that the worst would come. Anything was better than this uncertain state, not knowing but imagining so many frightful things. Even though I told myself that I didn't care, I knew inside that I did. For a while I even hoped that they could do something to my mind, somehow erase all my treasonous thoughts and make me content, like the boys around me.

130

I attended classes, went through the regular daily routines, ate, slept, and exercised, my mind in a constant, frightened turmoil.

Then the day came. There was a message for me at breakfast. I was to report to the director's office as soon as I finished my meal. With fear controlling my movements, I walked hesitantly down the long corridor and knocked at the door.

"Come in," the stern voice called.

I entered, again feeling smaller than I really was. But then some small measure of courage I hadn't known I possessed took over, and I remained standing before the man at the desk, willing to take whatever came.

"Your case has been reviewed," the director said, "and your fate has been decided. Are you sure, Steven, that you won't change your mind? Couldn't you be happy here and continue with things as they were before?"

Here was my chance. I wouldn't have to be shut up in an institution. I could live in the world and go to my job, and when the government decided on a mate for me, I could marry and probably have a child of my own. *To be what?* I asked

131

myself. *What will the government need, by the time I have a son, and what will they force him to do?*

"No, sir," I heard my voice say, and it sounded as if it came from some other person. "I couldn't."

The director looked a little sad. "Well, then," he said, "I'm afraid you'll have to leave us. Collect your things. You'll find a car waiting for you on the drive. I'm sorry to see you go, Steven, but I wish you good luck in the future. And, son," he said kindly, "who knows? Perhaps you are a scientist, after all."

"Thank you, sir," I said, puzzled by his words. The director wasn't really such a bad person. It wasn't his fault that things were as they were. He was simply doing his job. He seemed so distressed that I felt a little sorry for him.

I went back to the big room I had lived in for so long and shared with others of my kind. I had no idea where I would be going now, and I was sure that I would never see my parents again. Thinking of them almost made me change my mind. But no. I knew that they would be proud of my decision. Anything was better than this. I straightened my shoulders purposefully, took a last look around the room, picked up my bag, and strode out toward the unknown, appearing, I hoped, much braver than I felt.

A government limousine was pulled up next to the curb, with a uniformed chauffeur holding open the back door. I stifled a sob as I slid into the deep backseat of the big car, willing myself not to cry in front of the strange driver. Immediately, I realized that I was not alone in the backseat. I turned my head.

"Steven!" my father said, sliding over closer to my mother to make more room.

I gazed at them, dumbfounded. "Mom! Dad! What are you doing here?"

"We're so proud of you, son!" said Dad. He was smiling broadly.

"Y-You don't understand, Dad. I've been expelled. They're sending me away, and I don't even know where!"

Both my parents laughed delightedly. What was the matter with them? Were they glad that I was a misfit? I felt my eyes fill with tears.

My father sobered instantly, but there was still

133

laughter behind his eyes as he spoke. "Steven, Steven, it was all just a test! You should have suspected something when you were first sent to this school instead of one closer to home. We were under consideration for colonists all the time, but they had to be sure of you—"

"Dad," I broke in, "you still don't understand. I've failed your test!"

Mother leaned across Dad and laid her hand on mine. Her voice—and her eyes—were very serious. "Steven," she said, "what they had to be sure of was your courage to make the right decision. You obeyed your instincts and made the right choice, rebelling against the system and sticking with your decision, even with the danger of the unknown before you."

"You passed the test with flying colors," said Dad, his smile broad again. "We're going to New America—to be pioneers!"

TEDDI

by Andre Norton

JOBOY WAS STILL CRYING when the Little used
the stunner on him. Me, I had to lie there, with
that tangler cord around my feet, and watch.
Had to keep quiet, too. No use getting myself
blasted when maybe I could still take care of
Joboy.

"Take care of Joboy. . . ." I'd been hearing
that ever since he was born. Nats have to learn
to take care early, with Little hunting packs out
combing the hills and woods for them. Those
packs are able to pick off the Olds early, but in

135

the beginning, we kids aren't too much larger than the Littles, and we can hide out. We can't hide out forever, though. We have to eat, and in winter there isn't much to find in the hills—which means raiding down in Little country. Sooner or later, of course, we run into their traps, as Joboy and I did that night.

I was scared, sure, but I was more scared for Joboy. He had never been down in the fields before. I usually hid him out when I went food-snitching, but this time he had refused to stay behind. And then. . . .

All because of an old, dirty piece of fur stuffed with dried grass! I could have cried myself, only I wasn't going to let any Little see me do that. Joboy, he was just a kid, and it was his Teddi that had gotten us into this. I could see the darned thing now. One of the Littles had kicked it against the field wall, and now it sat there looking back at me, with that silly, stupid grin on its torn face.

Da had brought Teddi back to the cave when Joboy was still a baby. It was from the lowlands but not Little-made. Da told Joboy silly stories
136

about Teddi—kid stuff, but Joboy sure liked them. After Da went out that day and never came back, Joboy wanted me to tell them, too. First I tried to remember what Da had said. Then I just added extra things out of my own head. I think Joboy thought Teddi was alive. Once, when he got torn and lost some of his insides, Joboy went wild. I stuffed Teddi with grass and tried to patch him up, but I wasn't too good at it.

Joboy carried him all the time, but that night he dropped Teddi when I found the potatoes, and when he reached for him again, he set off the alarm, and the Littles were right on us.

They used a tangler on me quick. Guess they must have known I was a raider and knew most of the tricks. I told Joboy to beat it, and he might have gotten away if he hadn't tried to get Teddi again. So there we were; the Littles had us, but good.

Now they stood around us, looking us over as if we were animals. I guess, to the Littles, that's what we Nats were. I wondered if they knew just how much we hated them! Littles—I could have spit right in their nasty, screwed-up faces. Only

137

I didn't—not when they had Joboy and maybe would make him pay for what I did.

There were only six of them. Put me on my feet, free, and I could— But I knew I couldn't, ever. They had tanglers and stunners. What did we have? Stones and sticks. Da had had a gun but nothing left to shoot out of it. It was at the back of our cave now, leaning against the wall, not as much good as a well-shaped club would be.

The six of them were wearing the green suits of a hunting pack. They had come down on us in one of their copters. The Littles have everything—cars, planes, you name it—but we can't use them; they're all too small. Maybe Joboy could squeeze into the pilot's seat in a copter, but he wouldn't know how to fly it.

Joboy lay there as if he were dead, but he was only stunned—so far. I tried not to guess what they would do to us. We were Nats, and that made us things to be hunted down and gotten rid of.

A Little walked over to me and looked right down into my eyes. His eyes were cold and hard, like his face. Yet once we were the same, Littles
138

and Nats. They never seem to think of that, and I guess we don't much, either.

"You, Nat"—he nudged my shoulder with the toe of his boot—"where's your filthy nest? Any more of you back there?" I'm sure he didn't expect any answer. If he had dealt with us before, he should have known he would get none.

Da warned us long ago not to team up with any other Nats. More than one family of us together was easy hunting. Most of us stayed on our own. We were cautious about meeting strange Nats, too. Sometimes the Littles had tame Nats —ones they could control sent into the hill country to nose us out. However, no Nat ever spilled to the Littles unless he was brain-emptied, so the less we knew, the better. They might backtrack us to the cave, but that wouldn't do them any good. Da had been gone since last winter, and Mom, though I still remembered her, had died of the coughing sickness when Joboy was only a baby. Maybe they would find Da's hiding places and the books, but that didn't matter much at this point. They had us, and there was no escaping from a Nat pen, once you were dumped

139

in. Or was there? You heard stories, and I could keep my eyes and ears open. . . .

"No more of us," I told him truthfully. "Just Joboy and me."

He made a face as if I smelled bad. "Two's two too many. Sent for the pickup yet, Max?" He spoke to the one putting his stunner back in his belt after he had attended to Joboy.

"On its way, chief."

I wondered if I should cry a bit, let them see me scared. But then they might stun me, too. Better be quiet and try to find a way to— But there was no way. When I realized that, it was like really having the stunner knock me out, only I wasn't able to sleep. I had to lie and think about it.

They didn't pay me any more attention, because they didn't have to; that tangler held me as if I were shut up in a cave, with a rock too big to push filling the entrance. One of them wandered over to Teddi, laughed, and kicked him. Teddi sailed up in the air and came right apart at a seam. I was glad Joboy didn't see that, and I hated them worse than ever. I hated until

140

I was all hate and nothing else.

Pretty soon one of their trucks came along. The two men in the front got out. We were picked up, gingerly, as if the Littles hated even to touch us, and dumped in the back. I landed hard and it hurt, and I was glad Joboy couldn't feel it when he landed.

I had time to think as the truck ran along through the night, heading for one of their cities —cities that had once been ours, too. How long ago? I wondered.

Da could read the books. He could write, too. He made Joboy and me learn. Once he said that the Littles thought we were no better than animals, but that there was no need for us to prove them right. He made us learn about the past, as much as he knew.

Littles began quite a while back, when there were too many people in the world. The people built too many houses and too many roads, ate too much, and covered all the country. A lot of people began to worry, and they had different ideas as to what could help. The cities, especially, were traps, overpopulated and full of bad air.

141

None of their ideas seemed to work—until they started on the Littles. They found a way to work on a person's body, even before he was born, so that he started life a lot smaller and never did grow very big. His children were small, too, and so it went, on and on. The big cities now could house more and more people. They didn't have to build more and bigger roads, because the cars were made smaller and smaller, to match the Littles. Littles didn't need so much food, either, so less land was needed to produce what was required.

There were some people, however, who thought this was all wrong, and they refused to take the treatment to make their children little. When the government passed laws that said everyone *had* to be a Little, the Naturals—the Nats—moved to places where they thought they could hide. Then the Littles began to hunt them.

Da's people, way back, had been leaders against the idea of making Littles, because they had found out that being little began to change the way people thought, made them hate everyone not just like themselves. Da said they were

142

"conditioned" to have the ideas that those who were in power wanted them to have—like being a Little was the right way to live and being a Natural was like being a killer or a robber or something. Da said people had worked and fought and even died to let everyone have an equal chance in life, and now the Littles were starting the old, bad ways of thinking, all over again—only this time they were even worse.

That's why he held on to the old books and made us learn all about what had happened, so we could tell our children—though we probably wouldn't ever get to tell anyone anything now. I shivered as I bumped around in that truck, wondering what the Littles were going to do with us. They couldn't make us Littles, so what *did* they do with Nats when they caught them?

First they dumped us in a Nat pen. It was a big room, with walls like stone. Its small windows were so far up that there was no way to reach them. Along the walls were benches, squat and low, to match Littles and no one else. It smelled bad, as if people had been shut up there for a long time, and I guess people like us had

143

been. To the Littles, of course, we weren't people
—just things.

When the Littles brought us in, they had stunners out, and they yelled to the others to get
away from the door or they would ray. They
threw us on the floor, and then one sprayed the
tangler cords so they began to dissolve. By the
time I was free, the Littles were gone. I crawled
over to Joboy. Crawl was all I could do, I had
been tied up so long. Joboy was still sleeping. I
sat beside him and looked at the others in the
pen.

There were ten of them, all kids. A couple
were just babies, and they were crying. The only
one as old as me was a girl. She held one of the
babies, trying to get it to suck a wet rag, but she
looked over its head at me mighty sharp. There
were two other girls. The rest were boys.

"Tam?" Joboy opened his eyes. "Tam!" He
was scared.

"I'm here!" I put my hands on him so he'd
know it was the truth. Joboy had a lot of bad
dreams. Sometimes he woke up scared, and I had
to make him sure I was right there.

144

"Tam, where are we?" He caught at one of my hands with both of his and held it fast.

One of the boys laughed. "Look around, kid, just look around."

He was smaller than me, but now I saw he was older than I first thought. I didn't like his looks; he seemed too much like a Little.

He could be a "tweener." Some of the Little kids were what they called "throwbacks." They grew too big, so their people were ashamed and afraid of them and got rid of them. I guess they were afraid the tweeners might start everyone changing in size if they kept them around. The tweeners hated Nats, too—maybe even more, because they were something like them.

The girl with the baby spoke. "Shut up, Raul." Then she asked me, "Kinfolk?"

"Brothers." That Raul might be older, but I thought this girl was the head one there. "I'm Tam, and this is Joboy."

She nodded. "I'm El-Su. She's Amay." She motioned toward another girl, about Joboy's age, I reckoned, who had moved up beside her. "We're sisters. The rest. . . ." She said who they were,

145

but I didn't try to remember their names. They were mostly just dirty faces and ragged clothes.

I ran my tongue over my lips, but before I could ask any questions, Joboy jerked at my hand. "Tam, I'm hungry. Please, Tam—"

"What about it?" I turned to El-Su. "Do we get fed?"

She pointed to the other wall. "Sure. They don't starve us—at least, not yet. Go over there and press that red button. Be ready to catch what comes out, or it ends up on the floor."

I did as she told me, and it was a good thing she had warned me. As it was, I nearly didn't catch the pot of stuff. I took it over to one of the benches, Joboy tailing me. There were no spoons, so we had to eat with our fingers. The food was stewed stuff that didn't taste like much of anything, but we were hungry enough to scrape it all out. While we ate, the rest stood around watching us, as if they had nothing else to do—which was the truth.

When I had finished, I tried El-Su again.

"So they feed us. What else do they do? What do they want us for?"

146

Raul moved in between us and answered first. "Make you work, big boy—really make you work. Bet they haven't had one as big as you for a long time." He used the word "big" the way a Little does, meaning something nasty.

"Work how?" The Littles had machines to do their work, and those machines were made for Littles, not Nats, to run.

"You'll see—" Raul began, but El-Su, holding the baby, who had gone to sleep against her shoulder, reached out her other hand and gave him a push.

"He's asking me, *little* one." Now she made "little" sound nasty, in return. "They indenture us," she told me.

"Indenture?" That was a new word, and anything new, connected with Littles, could be bad. The sooner I knew how bad, the better.

She watched me closely, as if she thought I was pretending I didn't know what she meant.

"You never heard?"

I was short in answering. "If I had, would I be asking?"

"Right." El-Su nodded. "You must have been

147

picked up down south. Well, it's like this. The
Littles, they're sending ships up in the sky—way
off to the stars—"

"Moon walk!" One of Da's books had pictures
about that.

"Farther out." This El-Su spoke as if she had
had old books to read, too. "Clear to another sun
with a lot of worlds. To save space on the ship,
they put most of the people to sleep—freeze them
—until they get there."

Maybe if I hadn't read that book of Da's, I
would have thought she was making all this up
out of her head, the way I made up the stories
about Teddi for Joboy. But that moon book had
some talk in it about star travel, also.

"The Littles found a world out there, like this
one. But it's all wild—no cities, no roads, nothing—just lots of trees and country, where no one
has ever been. They want to live there, but they
can't take their digging and building machines
along. Those are too heavy; besides, they'd take
up too much room in the ship. So they want to
take Nats—like us—to do the work. They get
rid of grown-up Nats when they bring them here,

148

but they aren't so afraid of kids. Maybe we're lucky." El-Su didn't sound so sure about that, however.

"Yeah." Raul pushed ahead of her again. "You got to work and do just what a Little tells you to. And you'll never get back here, neither—not in your whole life! What do you think of that, big boy?"

I didn't think much of it, but I wasn't going to say so—not when Joboy had tight hold of my hand.

"Tam, are they really going to shoot us up into the sky?" he asked.

He didn't sound scared, as I thought he might be. He just looked interested when I glanced down at him. Joboy gets interested in things . . . likes to sit and study them. Back in the woods, he would watch bugs, for what seemed like hours, and then tell me what they were doing and why. Maybe he made it all up, but it sounded real. And he could chitter like a squirrel or whistle like a bird, until the animals would actually come to him.

"I don't know," I said, but I had no reason to

doubt that both El-Su and Raul *thought* they were telling the truth.

It seemed that they *were,* from what happened to us: After we had been there a couple of days, some Littles started processing us. That's what they called it—processing. We had to get scrubbed up, and they stuck us with needles. That hurt, but there was no getting back at them. Some of them had stunners, and even blasters, on us every minute. They never told us anything. That made it bad, because you kept thinking that something worse yet was waiting.

Then they divided the group. El-Su, Amay, and another girl, called Mara, Raul, Joboy, and me they kept together. I made up my mind that if they tried to take Joboy, stunner or no, I was going to jump the nearest Little. Perhaps the Littles guessed they would have trouble if they tried to separate us.

Finally they marched us into a place where there were boxes on the floor and ordered each of us to get into one. I was afraid for Joboy, but he didn't cry or hold back. He had that interested look on his face, and he even smiled at me. It gave me a warm feeling that he wasn't scared. I was—plenty!

We got into the boxes and lay down, and then, almost immediately, we went to sleep. I don't remember much, and I never knew how long we were in those boxes. For a while I dreamed. I was in a place all sunny and full of flowers with nice smells and lots of other happy things. There was Joboy, and he was walking hand in hand (or *paw* in hand) with Teddi. In that place, Teddi was as big as Joboy, and he was alive, as I think Joboy always thought he was.

They were talking without sounds—like just in their heads—and I could hear them, too. I can't remember what they were saying, except that it was happy talk. And I felt light and free, a way I couldn't remember ever feeling before— as if, in this place, you didn't have to be afraid of Littles or their traps. Joboy turned to look back at me, with a big smile on his face.

"Teddi knows. Teddi *always* knows," he said.

I hurt. I hurt all over. I hurt so bad I yelled; at least, somebody was yelling. I opened my eyes, and everything was all red, like fire, and that hurt, too—and so I woke up on a new world.

When we could walk (we were so stiff, it hurt to move at all), the Littles, four of them with blasters, herded us into another room, where the walls were logs of wood and the floor was dirt, tramped down hard. They made us take a bunch of pills, and we moved around, but there were no windows to see out of.

After a while, they came for us again and marched us out into the open. We knew then that we were on another world, all right.

The sky was *green*, not blue, and there were queer-looking trees and bushes. Right around the log-walled places, the ground had been burned off or dug up until it was typically ugly Little country. They had a couple of very small, light diggers and blasters, and they ran these around, trying to make the ugly part bigger.

We marched across to a place where there was just grass growing. There the Little chief lined us up and said this grass had to be dug out and cleared away so seeds could be planted, to test whether they could grow things from our world.

He had tools (they must have been made for tweeners, at least, because they were all right for us): shovels, picks, hoes. He told us to get to work.

It was tough going. The grass roots ran deep, and we couldn't get much of the ground scraped as bare as he wanted it. They had to give us breaks for rest and food. I guess they didn't want to wear us out too fast.

While we weren't working, I took every chance to look around. Once you got used to the different colors of things, it wasn't so strange. There was one thing, I think, that the Littles should have remembered better. We Nats had lived in the woods and wild places for a long time. We were used to trees and bushes. The Littles never liked to go very far into the wild places; they needed walls about them to feel safe and happy —if Littles could be happy.

So the wide bigness of this wild country must have scared the Littles. It bothered me, just because it was unfamiliar, but not as much as it bothered the Littles. I had a feeling that, if what lay beyond that big stand of trees was no worse

153

than what was right here, there was no reason why we Nats couldn't take to the woods the first chance we got. Then let the Littles just try to find us! I chewed on that in my mind but didn't say it out loud—yet.

It was on the fifth day of working that Raul, Joboy, and I were sent, along with a small clearing machine, in the other direction—into the woods on the opposite side of that bare place. I noticed that Joboy kept turning his head in one direction. When our guard dropped back, he whispered to me.

"Tam, Teddi's here!"

I missed a step. Teddi! Teddi was a dirty rag! Was Joboy hurt in the head now? I was so scared that I could have yelled, but Joboy shook his head at me.

"Teddi says no. He'll come when it's time. He don't like the Littles. They make everything bad."

They set us to piling up logs and tree branches. We could lift and carry bigger loads than any Little. I kept Joboy with me as much as I could, and away from Raul. I didn't want Raul to know about Joboy and Teddi. As far as I was con-

154

cerned, Raul still had some of the tweener look, and I never trusted him.

There was sticky sap oozing out of the wood, and it got all over us. At first I tried to wipe it off Joboy and myself, using leaves, but Joboy twisted away from me.

"Don't, Tam. Leave it on. It makes the bugs stay away."

I had noticed that the Littles kept slapping at themselves and grunting. There were a lot of flies, and from the way the Littles acted, they could really bite. But the buzzers weren't bothering us, so I was willing to stay sticky, if that's what helped. The Littles acted as if the bites were getting worse. They moved away from us. Finally two of them went back to the log buildings, to get bug spray, I suppose, leaving only the one who drove the machine. He got into the small cab and closed the windows. I suppose he thought there was no chance of our running off into that strange wilderness.

Raul sat down to rest, but Joboy wandered close to the edge of the cut, and I followed to keep an eye on him. He squatted down near a

155

bush, facing it. The leaves were big and flat and had yellow veins. Joboy stared, as if they were windows he could see through.

I knelt beside him. "What is it, Joboy?"

"Teddi's there." He pointed with his chin, not moving his scratched, dirty hands from his knees.

"Joboy—" I began, then stopped suddenly. In my head was something, not words but a feeling, like saying hello, except— Oh, I can never tell just how it was!

"Teddi," Joboy said. His voice was like Da's, when I was no older than Joboy and there was a bad storm and Da was telling me not to be afraid.

What made that come into my mind? I stared at the bush. As I studied it now, I saw an opening between two of the leaves that *was* a window, enough for me to see—

Teddi! Well, perhaps not Teddi as Da had first brought him (and before Joboy wore him dirty and thin from much loving) but enough like him to make Joboy know. Only this was no stuffed toy; this was a live creature! And it was fully as large as Joboy himself, which was about

156

as big as one of the Littles. Its bright eyes stared straight into mine.

Again I had that feeling of greeting, of meeting someone who meant no harm, who was glad to see me. I had no doubt that this was a friend. But—what was it? The Littles hated wild things, especially *big* wild things. They would kill it! I glanced back at the one in the cab, almost sure I would see him aiming a blaster at the bush.

"Joboy," I said as quietly as I could, "the Little will—"

Joboy smiled and shook his head. "The Little won't hurt Teddi, Tam. Teddi will help us; he likes us. He *thinks* to me how he likes us."

"What you looking at, kid?" Raul called.

Joboy pointed to a leaf. "The buzzer. See how big that one is?"

Sure enough, there was an extra-big one of the red buzzing flies sitting on the leaf, scraping its front legs together and looking as if it wanted a bite of someone. At that moment, I felt Teddi leave, which made me happier, as I didn't have Joboy's confidence in Teddi's ability to defend himself against the Littles.

That was the beginning. Whenever we went near the woods, sooner or later Teddi would turn up in hiding. I seldom saw any part of him, but I always felt him come and go. Joboy seemed to be able to *think* with him and exchange information—until the day Teddi was caught.

The creature had always been so cautious that I had begun to believe that the Littles would never know about him. But suddenly he walked, on his hind legs, right into the open. Raul yelled and pointed, and the Little on guard used his stunner. Teddi dropped. At least, he hadn't been blasted, not that that would necessarily save him.

I expected Joboy to go wild, but he didn't. He went over with the rest of us to see Teddi, lying limp and yellow on mashed, sticky leaves where we had been taking off tree limbs. Joboy acted as if he didn't know a thing about him. That I could not understand.

Teddi was a little taller than Joboy. His round, furry head would just top my shoulder, and his body was plump and fur-covered all over. He had large, round ears, set near the top of his head, a muzzle that came to a point, and a dark brown

158

button of a nose. Yes, he looked like an animal, but I was sure he was something far different.

Now he was just a stunned prisoner, and the Littles made us carry him over to the machine. Then they took us all back to camp. They dumped us in the lockup and took Teddi into another hut. I know what Littles do to animals. They might— I only hoped Joboy couldn't imagine what the Littles might do to Teddi. I still didn't understand why he wasn't upset.

But when we were shut in, he took my hand. "Tam?"

I thought I knew what he was going to ask— that I help Teddi—and there was nothing I could do.

"Tam, listen—Teddi, he wanted to be caught. He did! He has a plan for us. It will work only if he gets real close to the Littles, so he had to be caught."

"What does he mean?" El-Su demanded.

"The kid's mind-broke!" Raul burst out. "They knocked over some kind of an animal out there and—"

"Shut up!" I snapped at Raul. I had to know

160

what Joboy meant, because it was plain that he believed what he was saying, and he knew far more about Teddi than I did.

"Teddi can do things with his head." Joboy paid no attention to either El-Su or Raul, looking straight at me as if he must make me believe what he was saying.

Remembering for myself, I could agree in part. "I know—"

"He can make them—the Littles—feel bad inside. But we have to help."

"How? We can't get out of here—"

"Not yet," Joboy agreed. "But we have to help Teddi think—"

"Mind-broke!" Raul exploded and slouched away. But El-Su and the other two girls squatted down to listen.

"How do we help think?" She asked the question already on my tongue.

"You feel afraid. Remember all the bad things you are afraid of. And we hold hands in a circle to remember them—like bad dreams." Joboy was plainly struggling to find words to make us understand.

161

"That's easy enough—to remember bad things," El-Su agreed. "All right, we think. Come on, girls." She took Amay's hand and Mara's. I took Mara's other hand, and Joboy took Amay's, so we were linked in a circle.

"Now"—Joboy spoke as sharply as any Little setting us to work—"think!"

We had plenty of bad things to remember: cold, hunger, fear. Once you started thinking and remembering, it all heaped up into a big black pile of bad things. I thought about every one of them—how Mom died, how Da was lost, and how—and how—and how. . . .

I got so I didn't even see where we were or whose hands I held. I forgot all about the present; I just sat and remembered and remembered. It came true again in my mind, as if it were happening all over again, until I could hardly stand it. Yet once I had begun, I had to keep on.

Far off, there was a noise. Something inside me tried to push that noise away. I had to keep remembering, feeding a big black pile. Then suddenly the need for remembering was gone. I awakened from the nightmare.

162

I could hear someone crying. El-Su was facing me with tear streaks on her grimy face; the two little girls were bawling out loud. But Joboy wasn't crying. He stood up, looking at the door, though he still held on to our hands.

Then I looked in that direction. Raul crouched beside the door, hands to his head, moaning as if something hurt him bad. The door was opening—probably a Little, to find out why we were making all that noise.

Teddi stood there, with another Teddi behind him, looking over his shoulder. All the blackness was gone out of my head, as if I had rid myself of all the bad that had ever happened to me in my whole life. I felt so light and free and happy —as if I could flap my arms like wings and go flying off!

Outside, near where the Teddis stood, there was a Little crawling along the ground, holding on to his head the way Raul did. He didn't even see us as we walked past him. We saw two other Littles, one lying quiet, as if he were dead. Nobody tried to stop us or the Teddis. We just walked out of the bad old life together.

163

I don't know how long we walked before we came to an open place, and I thought, *This I remember, because it was in my dream.* Here were Joboy and Teddi, hand in paw. There was a Teddi with me, too, his furry paw in my hand, and from him the feeling was all good.

We understand now what happened and why. When the Littles first came to this world, spoiling and wrecking, as they always have done and still do, the Teddis tried to stop them. But the minds of the Littles were closed tight; the Teddis could not reach them—not until they found Joboy. He had no fear of them, because he knew a Teddi who had been a part of his life.

So Joboy was the key to unlock the Littles' minds, with us to add more strength, just as it takes more than one to lift a really big stone. With Joboy and us opening the closed doors of the Littles' minds, the Teddis could feed back to them all the fear they had spread through the years, the fear we had lived with and known in our nightmares. Such fear was a poison worse than any of the Littles' own weapons.

We still go and *think* at them now and then,

164

with a Teddi to aim our thoughts from where we hide. From all the signs, it won't be long before they will have had enough and will raise their starship and leave us alone. Maybe they will try to come back, but by then, perhaps, the Teddis and we can make it even harder for them.

Now we are free, and no one is ever going to put us back in a Nat pen. We are not "Nats" anymore. That is a Little name, and we take nothing from the Littles—ever again! We have a new name from old, old times. Once it was a name to make little people afraid, so it is our choice. We are free, and we are *Giants*, growing larger every day.

So shall we stay!

IT'S SO WONDERFUL HERE *by Bill Pronzini*

IT'S SO WONDERFUL HERE.

There's soft golden sunshine every day, and the air is warm and spicy-sweet. We have a stream on our parcel, with icy water that tingles your toes and makes them numb when you go wading. There's lots of shade, too, and fruit trees and thick green grass and hundreds of different kinds of flowers—some almost my size, with bright pink petals you can use to make kites.

Kite flying is fun, and so is chasing orange and black singing butterflies across the meadows or stretching out on one of the knolls to watch our twin moons bounce up like funny white balls, just after sunset. Oh, there's just so much you can do here! You can pick joyberries along the banks of Big Winding River, beyond where our stream joins it a mile from here; or you can hide and watch the fisher-birds that live on the Yamashitas' parcel, building their nests and hunting catchpennies in the river; or you can go exploring in the Big Wood that stretches for miles and miles and separates all the parcels of land in A-section from City.

I like the Big Wood best of all, I think. I know all the paths, and I can go in way deep, where it's dark and the tree branches are so thick overhead that you can't even see the sky. It smells green and moist and fresh in there, and you don't have to worry about animals or anything, because there's nothing in the Big Wood except the gehas—and they're friendlier than the kitten I once had, back on Earth, and softer, too, and funnier to watch when they roll themselves into furry little balls and hide among the leaves.

Selena and I went into the Big Wood this

167

morning to hunt for thryax. Selena's my best friend. She lives with her parents on the parcel next to ours; she's eleven and a half, and I'm just four months younger. She has more chores to do than I have, because her parents are pretty strict, but this morning they let her come to the Big Wood because they went to the airport in City with my mom and dad and some of the other grown-ups in A-section. There's a ship coming in from Earth today, the first one in a long time, and whenever a ship comes in from Earth, all the grown-ups get pretty excited and don't pay much attention to us kids. They used to take us along to see the ship come down and unload and to listen to the stories and the news the Spacers had to tell. But most of us aren't much interested in the ships or the port anymore, and the Spacers always bring awful stories from Earth, and the grown-ups just stand around looking as if the bad news is somehow their fault. Anyway, they let us stay at home now, and they go to City by themselves. There's nothing on this world that can hurt anybody, so they never have to worry about our being alone.

168

We spent the whole morning in the Big Wood, Selena and I, and we found lots of thryax where the cool green moss grows, way in deep. Thryax are a sort of funny purple color, but they're really good to eat. Mom says they taste a little like mushrooms, only better, but I don't know. I don't remember about mushrooms, if I ever even ate any on Earth.

We came out of the Big Wood, carrying our buckets of thryax, at one o'clock. I can tell time by the position of our sun; that's how I knew it was one o'clock. We started off across the meadow toward my house, picking yellow long-bells and pulling them in our hair, which made us feel beautiful. Pretty soon I could see the house, and there was smoke coming out of the big stone chimney on one side.

"My mom and dad are home," I said to Selena. "Mom likes a fire, even if it's warm. She says it reminds her of home."

"I suppose my parents are home, too. I'd better go and see what chores they have for me."

"Maybe they won't have any. Sometimes they don't when they've been to City and the port to

169

see one of the Earth ships. You know how they always act after they've talked to the Spacers."

"That's right!" Selena said. "Maybe we can go wading later on, then."

"And afterward, we'll fly our petal kites."

"I'll bring mine when I come. 'Bye, Hope."

" 'Bye, Selena."

She hurried off toward her house, and I went on through the meadow and across our vegetable field with my bucket of thryax. Our house is just about like all the others in A-section, because the men built them that way, one right after another, just after we came here. It's made of logs and stones, with stone floors inside, even in my little bedroom, and I love it. It's much nicer than the house we had back on Earth, at least as I remember that one.

Mom and Dad were sitting at the big wooden table in the center of the main room, in front of the fireplace, when I came in. They both looked up at me. I could see shiny streaks down Mom's cheeks, and I knew she'd been crying again. I went over to her, feeling unhappy all of a sudden, as I always do when Mom cries.

"Hope, honey," she said and hugged me tight. "Oh, baby, baby, baby."

"What is it, Mom? What's the matter?"

"It's nothing, dear."

She let me go and rubbed at her eyes with her fists, the way the gehas in the Big Wood do sometimes; but it wasn't funny the way Mom did it—not at all. I put my arm around her and looked at Dad. "Did you see the Earth ship?" I asked him.

"Yes, Hope, we saw the Earth ship."

"How come they were so late getting here this time?"

Dad's face had pain in it that he couldn't hide, and that made me unhappy, too. "Things on Earth are very bad now, honey," he said. "Worse than ever."

"Will there be any more ships?"

"I don't know. Maybe . . . maybe there won't. Probably not, I guess."

"Well," I said, "it's not really important, is it?"

They looked at me as if they were shocked and scared and sad, all at once, but they didn't say anything; they just looked at me that way. I knew

I'd said the wrong thing, but I didn't know what —not exactly. "I guess I'd better go and clean these thryax for supper. Selena and I found them in the Big Wood today."

"Yes," Dad said, "you do that, Hope."

I went into the pantry and filled a big wooden bowl with some of the water Dad carries up from the stream every morning. I began to wash and clean the thryax. I could hear Mom and Dad talking out in the main room, but I couldn't hear what they were saying. Finally I finished with the thryax and put the bowlful of them in one of the cool floor cupboards. When I came back into the main room, Mom and Dad stopped talking. There were still tearstains on Mom's cheeks, and Dad's eyes were still filled with pain.

I looked down at my bare feet and asked, "Do you have any more chores for me to do? The thryax are all cleaned and ready to cook."

"No," Dad said. "No, you run along and play now, Hope."

"All right."

I lifted my head and smiled at them, to let them know I was sorry for what I'd said, whatever it

173

was. Then I went outside. But when I passed the window, I could hear them talking again inside. Mom said, "She doesn't understand, John. She just doesn't understand. She only knows 'it's so wonderful here.' "

"Maybe it's just as well," Dad said.

"I don't know . . . I don't know." Mom's voice was getting higher and louder. "It's been more than seven years since we came here, John—but it seems like seventy. It seems like seven hundred —seven hundred years of nothing to struggle for and earn, because it's already 'so wonderful here'!"

"Yes," Dad said, and his voice sounded all thick and funny. "Yes, Karen, I know."

Mom was crying again. "I wish we could go home. How I wish we could go home!" Mom was silent for a minute; then she said, so softly that I could hardly hear her, "Maybe we should *all* go home. Maybe we could undo what we let happen to our world. Maybe we could make it wonderful *there* again, too. At least we'd have something to work for—"

"Karen, don't! You know we can't," Dad said,

174

and Mom began to sob again.

I went away from the window, toward Selena's house. I don't like to listen to Mom cry. And it's worse because I really *don't* understand, just as she said. I don't understand at all when they go to the port and come back and talk that way and Mom cries. *Home* is a terrible place. I was only four when we left in the ship, and I don't remember much about it, but I've seen tri-dim photos the Spacers brought, and it's just awful there. The trees and flowers and plants are all dead, and it's thick gray all the time, with no sunshine, and you can't breathe without an Oxy over your mouth and nose. That's why almost everyone has left to come out to a world like this one. That's why *we* came.

I just don't understand Mom and Dad and all the other grown-ups who act as if they're home-sick or something—or as if they'd even done wrong to come here in the first place.

Why would anyone want to go back to a place like Earth, when it's so wonderful here?

THE LITTLE MONSTER

by Poul Anderson

THROUGHOUT THAT TERRIBLE end-of-night, Jerry Parker kept his head. Once he even called skyward, "Hey, Mr. Matthews, if I last this thing out, I ought to make Eagle, huh?" But his Scoutmaster was a million and a half years away in time. So were Dad, Mother, Sis. . . .

A long-drawn roar coughed and thundered over plains white beneath a sinking moon, under stars wheeling, frosty, in nameless constellations. The noise was followed by a series of yelps, a cackling scream. Unseen wings were ghostly

176

above him. If nothing of him came home, except his clean-picked bones. . . .

He hunched, hugging himself, in what little shelter from the cold a spiny bush offered. His clothes were only sport shirt, lightweight slacks, sneakers. Teeth clattered in his head. Spain of the Pliocene Period— No, wait; this land didn't look right for Spain—not the topography nor the wildlife nor— Well, Europe was supposed to be warmer now than in 1995. The Ice Age hadn't begun. If Earth had any polar caps at all, they were not large. That meant less rainfall in these parts, and no forests. Open grasslands would get hot enough by day but chill off fast after sundown.

Was this also true in Ohio, which didn't yet exist? He couldn't tell. He was no geologist; he was only a boy who, for a twelfth-birthday present, had been (would be?) sent to spend a summer with the family of his Spanish mother's brother.

Ohio . . . Dad, Mother, Sis, the dogs, his friends and schoolmates, his teachers and Scout troop, his books and carpentry bench . . . gentle countrysides, gleaming cities, aircars murmuring through the heavens . . . a vacation trip to Rio and a telecast from Mars—all unborn, non-existent, unimaginable. He couldn't even call any of them very clearly to mind. How could the image of his father strengthen or the image of his mother comfort, when they would not even *be* for fifteen thousand centuries?

Somehow, Jerry found, he could more readily hark back to his uncle's laboratory, though, in a way, that crowded apparatus, those oracular meters, the technicians at their enigmatic work, seemed as alien as the land which now held him.

"Never mind the physics of it," Antonio Viana said. He spoke excellent English; but then, he was world-renowned for his contribution in bringing Mitsuhito's theory of temporal relativistics into engineering practice. "Come back when you know tensor calculus, and I'll explain to you about n-dimensional forces and the warping of world lines. Today I thought you would simply like to visit the shop."

"Oh, gee, would I ever!" Jerry breathed. He

hesitated. "Of course, I've read a lot about time projection, and I've seen things on TV, but your place never was mentioned. I've never actually been in a lab. . . ."

A smile flashed through Uncle Antonio's beard. "True, we have attracted no foreign newsmen, but ours is a small, rather specialized part of an international effort. We have had no spectacular results so far—or, rather, the anthropologists we have been sending back have had none."

"They haven't seen any, uh, cavemen?" Jerry asked.

Uncle Antonio chuckled. "Not hereabouts. Besides, no one ever will, strictly speaking, unless we can find a way to enter the past at a later date than about one million B.C. There were no men that early—only ancestral half-apes." He shrugged. "Not that I am an anthropologist myself. I am just a physicist and engineer, but, helping to send expeditions back, I grew interested. I asked questions and read books."

"Well, how come they haven't even met any, uh, half-apes?"

"A protohuman, or the original Homo sapiens,

179

for that matter, was a rare animal, Jerry. Suppose you, today, had about thirty hours to fish off the coast of Africa. How likely would you be to catch a coelacanth?" The man paused. "Besides, the temporal inertia effect does more than bar us from the closer past and bar us completely from the future. It also causes great uncertainty about arrival dates. As near as can be checked by astronomical instruments—not very near, considering how the skies change over so much time—no two expeditions have landed even within thousands of years of each other. We know, from fossils, that premen once lived in this neighborhood, but we don't know exactly when, and we have never happened to hit it right. You cannot possibly hope to search a wide area in thirty hours, either."

"Will they ever manage to improve that?" Jerry wondered.

"Well, we are trying," Uncle Antonio said. "You see us experimenting, hoping to get more precision. I do not think we will lengthen the time span that can be spent in the past. What we send is snapped back to here and now after
180

thirty hours, because of built-up stresses in the continuum. That is also the reason our people cannot bring anything home with them except photographs, notes—essentially the same matter as they took along."

"Hey, look," Jerry protested, since this had never been made clear to him, "the men you've sent have sampled water and fruits and all kinds of things in the past. They've certainly breathed the air. What about the atoms their bodies took up and the other atoms they got rid of?"

The man rumpled the boy's brown hair. "A good brain under that mop," he said, laughing. Again he shrugged, in his very Latin way. "I think maybe the intermolecular forces account for it—that people do come back whole, with full lungs and so on, I mean. Maybe this will give us an approach to collecting objects, live plants, animals. Temporalistics is still such a new science. Many unknowns."

They had stopped before a burnished steel cylinder, studded with instruments and controls, on which a pair of technicians labored. A window showed a bare interior. "We project the travelers

181

from this," Uncle Antonio said. "Would you like to step inside?"

A thrill ran through Jerry. "Gosh, thanks!" He darted through the open door.

The chamber was narrow and cheerless—but nevertheless exciting to Jerry. Trying to capture a sense of really going off on a time voyage, he started to close the door.

He barely glimpsed a horrified face in the window, barely heard a screamed *"No, no!"* He couldn't stop his motion fast enough. The heavy metal door clanged shut.

Then came the flash, the whirling, the. . . .

First light. Wind cold over skin, ruffle hair, whistle from gray-before-sun till stars go. Dew shiny on thorn wall, tree leaf; wet smell. Nest rustle soggy. Warm bodies, flesh smell, dry grass smell, mold-underneath smell.

Lion smell!

Last night lion prowl outside thorn wall. Roar. Lion alone. Hes wake, grab spears, jump around shes and cubs, scream, show teeth. Lion go. He-lion; see mane under moon. Lame. Big, big, big.

Come back tonight? Help, Old Father!

Get up. Cubs cry; mothers give milk. Thirsty. Hungry. Lion. . . . Thirsty. Hungry. Go to water hole. Go hunt.

Old Father's pole bent over outside thorn wall. Lion hit it with clawpaw. Untangle branches. Scratch. Blood on skin. Go out. Straighten pole. Reach; daub blood from scratch onto Old Father's teeth. Howl for Old Father; dance before his hollow eyes. All hes howl, dance. Old Father, do not call lion back! We feed you!

Ung-ng-n-n-n. To water hole. Hes outside band, with sharpstones and spears. Half-cubs inside hes, with rocks and clubs. Inside them, shes and cubs. Flesh smell. Breathing, chattering, shoving. Walk through tall, whispery, yellow grass to water hole.

Sunup. Sky, hills blue. Antelope herd far off by mimosa trees. Pride of lions come back from kill. Quick, make ring—spears outward, jump, bellow, bristle hair, whiskers! Lions look sleepy at us; go on. Hale lion not hunt man. Limping lion hunt man.

These lions kill last night. Leave carcass.

Where? Look. Vultures coming down yonder. Quick, before hyenas. Hurry to water hole.

Khr-r-rarr. Mastodon drinking. Must wait in woods. Hear splash, slurp, belly-rumble. Find grubs in rotten log. Sweet. Groom each other. Catch fleas; crack between teeth.

Mastodon go away; hill-high. Branches swish around flanks. Out on savannah, mastodons' hair red under sun, tusks old-bone-white. Smell rank. Grass crushed under feet smell sweet.

To water hole. Muddy. Taste, smell like bottom ooze. Drink fast; aaaahh! Not stop to chase frogs. Carcass waiting.

Back to thorn wall. Shes, cubs, half-cubs stay near here; search for roots, worms, grasshoppers; maybe knock over hare with flung stone. Old Father, keep lame lion asleep by day!

Hes go to kill of lions. Lope over plain. Hot. Grass brush skin, rustle, ripple. Breeze bring meat smell. Vultures, flies thick ahead. Big Kill. Horse? Elk? Hold sharpstone tight. Sharpstones to rip skin, cut carcass apart. Hes to bring home bones, to cut off meat, lovely fat. To crack bones with rock, suck lovely marrow. . . .

184

Vultures flap away.

Howls like laughing. Harsh smell. Shaggy, high-shouldered bodies. Hyena pack on way.

Skulk off. Man band can't fight hyenas. Look for small game. Spear can't break thick skins like lion claw, leopard jaw, sabertooth. Man band hunt anteater, hare, coney, snake, lizard; maybe catch young of big game.

Carcass smell lovely. Hyenas laugh. Man band go.

Hungry, hungry.

Dawn stole up above eastern hills. Jerry stretched stiffened limbs and jogged around the bush to start his blood moving warmly.

With waxing daylight, nightmarishness faded. He could understand what had happened. Probably the workers had had the main circuits closed but the fail-safe devices disconnected while they tinkered, and they had neglected to tell their chief. Closing the door had tripped the last switch needed to activate the projector.

You couldn't blame the technicians too much; they had assumed that whoever entered that

185

chamber would know. Also, he, Jerry, should have asked before touching anything.

"Well, never mind whose fault it was," he said aloud into the wind. "I'm here—or should I say I'm *now?*"

The area was a suburb of Valladolid, A.D. 1995, but in present reality, it was dry savannah under a cruelly bright sun, 1,500,000 B.C., give or take enough millennia that there was no possibility of sending him help.

In thirty-odd hours, minus the few he'd already spent, he would return to 1995. It would be not only to almost the exact moment of departure, but also to the exact spot, even if he wandered around in the meantime—so he might as well.

In fact, he'd better. Some of those animals in the dark had sounded awfully mean. He had no shelter here, no tree to climb, no weapon better than his Scout knife.

Suppose he died. His body would still return. Suppose it were eaten. Would anything enter the chamber except bones? Jerry shivered and struck off northward, merely because that kept the low sun out of his eyes.

186

It rose as he walked, and the heat increased. Crickets leaped and chirped. The land reached on and on, in billows of tawny grass that soughed in the faint breezes. At a distance, he spied an immense, earth-darkening herd. He couldn't make out what kinds of animals were in it— more than one kind, surely—apart from a few that were elephants, but not quite. These trumpeted, a somehow shrill bass that rolled across the grassland. The cloudless, pale blue sky filled with wings and became clamorous with voices.

Thirst nagged Jerry. He said aloud, just to hear something human, "That much life has to have water. I can last without it, but a drink'd be nice. Mainly, though, a river or a spring ought to mean trees that I could roost in after sundown. . . ."

When at last, afar, he saw low, scattered growths, it was noon. He rested. Peering northeast, he made out a dim line on the horizon. A grove? Worth trying. He trudged on through late afternoon.

Yes, those were stunted trees with dusty green foliage, clustered around what must be a water

187

hole. Individual trees were strung out across the plain. One of them, some two miles from the woods, stood by itself but was fairly tall. It seemed to be surrounded by— Was it a lot of the scrubby thornbush that grew everywhere about? No, not exactly. Hard to tell, with this early evening light, these long shadows, his own thirst and hunger and weariness. . . .

A line of animals was headed toward it, evidently returning from a drink. They were silhouetted black against the fading light. Jerry gulped and pulled out his knife. He couldn't really see them in detail, but didn't they walk upright?

A wind gusted at his back. Suddenly a chorus of harsh yells burst over him. Members of the band came leaping, howling, chattering their teeth. Their bodies were the bodies of small, dark, wiry, naked men, and they brandished crudely shaped sticks and stones. Their heads were the heads of beasts.

Stop! What? Man smell?
Man coming yonder?

No strange man on our grounds! Drive outsider away! Hes lope close, yell, jump around, make afraid. Kyaa, kyaa, kyaa!

No man, this. No ape—two legs. No man. Smell wrong. Look wrong. Bigger than a she, not as big as a he. Short hair, no whiskers, flat face, thin jaw, no fangs. Hand hold shiny sharpstone. Backing off. Sweating in chill breeze. Stinking of fear.

Kyaa, kyaa, kyaa! Food!

Rush. Monster turn around, run. Hear breath sob in, out. Slow he run. Throw sharpstone. *Thunk* between shoulders! Monster stumble, fall, Surround. Move in for kill.

Monster spring up. Rush in under spear. Shriek. Slash. Shiny sharpstone cut arm open to bone. Blood, hurt, yammer. Monster has sharp, sharp sharpstone. Monster slash next he.

Draw back. Bristle, spread lips, clack teeth, growl, beat breast. Monster stand fast. Smell monster's fear. Throw another stone. Monster catch with free hand, throw back. Owwww! Blood run into eyes, mouth. Hot, salt-sweet.

Monster retreat. Hes not follow. Shes, cubs

yelling, scared. Sun on world edge. Lame lion come soon? Move backward, shake weapons, growl, flash teeth at standing monster.

Monster follow, not close. Stop again. Here thorn wall. Part branches. Scratches? Not like sharp, sharp sharpstone! Everybody go inside. Passing by Old Father, crawl. Old Father, help! Drive away big lion, little monster.

Close thorn wall. Keep watch. Hack day's catch apart. Coney, snake, lizard, field mouse, field mouse, field mouse, toad, handful crickets. Hungry tonight. Lion pride not hungry. Hyenas not hungry. Man band not have sharp claws, big jaws. Hes, shes, half-cubs hungry. Lame lion hungry. Old Father, help!

Peer out through dusk. Monster by tree yonder. Pulling grass? Breaking branches? Squat and chip rock? Hard to see. Dark getting thick.

Lion roar, boom-boom-br-r-room.

By monster—red, yellow, crackle, smoke sting. *Fire!* Howl fear. Old Father, Old Father!

Pithecanthropus, Jerry thought. And again, aloud, out of a dry mouth into a gathering wind

and deepening shadows: "I had to be the one to stumble on preman. Not a scientific expedition, but me—and I p-p-pretty near got killed and eaten, I guess."

His self-defensive fight had been sheer terror reflex. It was blurred in his memory. He didn't know why the males hadn't pressed their attack. They could have taken him. His knife had inflicted no serious wounds. He wasn't able to field every thrown rock. Those pointed sticks weren't much as spears, but they'd have hurt him, and once he was down, he could have been clubbed to death.

Maybe his strangeness had made them hold back. From Scouting and natural history books, he knew that carnivores don't look for unnecessary trouble. Courage is a human invention. Beasts of prey want nothing except to stay alive; they seldom tangle with any creature that has a chance to harm them. And you couldn't call those —those monsters there—human!

Besides, they'd seemed anxious to get themselves and their mates and young inside that crude low wall of thorny boughs. They probably didn't dare to get caught in the open after dark. A big cat. . . .

"And you'd better not loaf around, either," Jerry told himself. "Pick a tree, while you've still got light to see by." There would be a moon, but not till an hour or two after sunset, and meanwhile dimness stole out of the west. Sometime tomorrow morning, the stresses were supposed to discharge and carry him home—but he had to last until then.

He threw a tortured glance toward the water hole. No telling what might lurk in that now-gloomy grove. Parched tongue and painfully empty stomach he could tough out. Be nice to have a fire, though. Protection, too.

No really good refuge tree was in reach before nightfall, except the one the ape-folk had taken. Jerry chose the best of a bad lot, a gnarled thing whose twigs ripped at him when he tested climbing it. He got about thirteen feet aloft before the limbs grew too weak. That was useless against an arboreal hunter like a leopard; even a determined lion might leap high enough to pluck him down. "Better build a fire—fast!" he muttered.

193

Luckily, fuel lay around: punk for tinder, bark and grass for kindling, larger wood from a nearby dead tree, ample dry dung. To start a fire without matches was a problem. Jerry scurried around, squinting into the dusk, which relentlessly closed around him.

He found a good many smallish stones. Most were shards or other stones bearing signs of workmanship. The ape-folk did chip an edge and a rough shape from a rock. The result was an unspecialized tool, equally useful (or semiuseful) for casting as a weapon, for butchering prey, and for scraping out a point of sorts on a stick, which would then serve as a blunt, soft spear.

Through gray blueness that hid the horizon, a roaring drummed. Jerry heard an answering clamor, high and terrified, from behind the ring of thorn branches. Iciness crawled up his own spine and over his scalp. Somehow he forced himself to continue his search in the grass.

There—what he'd hoped for! Not flint, to use with the steel of his pocketknife, but at least a chunk of pyrite, its golden hue barely visible in the last illumination. Squatting by his tinder, he held it in his left hand and clashed another stone against it. For a moment his heart halted; nothing had happened. He began to tremble. "Stop that!" he told himself and gave another, more glancing blow. Sparks flew, as brilliant as hope.

He managed a strained grin. "Thanks, Mr. Matthews," he whispered, as if his Scoutmaster were there and could hear. Woodcraft; primitive lore, including ways of fire making; the incidental information that pyrite was abundant in Spain. . . .

Crouch close, smite shower after shower of sparks onto the tinder. See one catch and glow, ever so faintly. Puff. Too hard; out it went. Try again.

When the first twigs crackled, when his fire really was started, Jerry cried. He couldn't help himself.

The lion bawled again, closer. Invisible, save as a bulk of blackness underneath early stars, the ape-folk's camp chattered forlorn defiance. Jerry threw a glance their way.

"I hope he d-d-does eat you," he half sobbed. "You filthy cannibals!"

Then somehow the thought that these were *his, Jerry Parker's,* noble ancestors, or so close as to make no difference, and that he might have become their dinner, struck him as insanely funny. He shrieked laughter, until renewed lion thunder brought him up short with the knowledge of how near to hysteria he had come.

"A spear is a great idea," he breathed shakily. From his tree, he cut a stout, not too crooked branch, almost as long as he was. It took time, even with a steel blade, but he had nothing else to do.

Often he needed to pause to feed the fire, which had become sizable—his friend, dancing, sputtering, casting a smoky glow toward the stars . . . many-colored flames that sang and drove the night back into demon-shaped shadows.

Cross-legged, Jerry whittled a point on the stave and reasonable straightness into its length. Next he fire-hardened the point, turning it round and round over the coals till the wood dried to black toughness. Always he was aware of unseen eyes watching from behind the thorns.

His thoughts ran on as if he still spoke to himself or to Uncle Antonio or his father: *I sure understand why people used to hate to think they were descended from creatures like those. I don't care much for the idea, either.*

In body they were human enough, erect and not especially hairy. Of course, they were runts, the biggest adult male little more than about five feet tall. Their nude hides were weathered to a leathery brown; on some, in that first flashing instant of encounter, he had noticed signs of skin disease. Their heads, topped by greasy black manes, were small, with little brow but with thick ridges over the eyes. They had flat noses and powerful-looking jaws. The males' beards and throat ruffs concealed what was obvious on the females and the young: that there was little or no chin.

The band numbered perhaps ten adults of each sex and twenty half-grown offspring. Three or four of the females had clutched infants. The infant mortality must be too high to bear thinking about (Jerry didn't suppose the ape-folk were capable of thinking about it), and certainly no one lived to be old. Doubtless this band were as

197

many as the whole grim country within sight would support.

"I guess you can't blame them for trying to drive a stranger out of their territory," Jerry said to himself. "But they didn't just make a threat display, as normal animals would. They wanted to kill me. They're cannibals! Why else do they keep, outside that fence, on a pole, the skull of one of their own kind?"

He shuddered and longed miserably for dawn. Only the moon rose, cold and lopsided above the swiftly chilling air. It turned the grasslands hoar, save where bushes and trees made misshapen darknesses, the ape-folk's camp a bigger one. Jerry huddled closer to his fire.

Its heat was like a caress. He was tired, so tired; drowsiness rolled over him in thick, soft waves; he'd better climb. . . .

The lion woke him.

He was into his tree before the roar and the shrieks had fully registered. Clinging to a limb, he stared across fifty yards, his vision sharpened by terror.

His fire had burned low, to a mere heap of sullen red and tiny bluish flickers. Nonetheless, it had doubtless made the beast avoid him. Moonlight and uncountable stars turned the savannah into an ice-colored lake. His heart pounding uncontrollably, Jerry imagined that he could actually count the ribs of the lion.

The animal was truly that gaunt—a male whose mane was ragged and whose coat was mangy. He limped, his right hind paw a mass of infection from some injury. His voice boomed, hollow and desperate.

In their compound, the ape-folk yammered. From his perch, Jerry could see that the females had borne their young into the high tree. They clustered there like ungainly fruit. No room remained, save in the lowest boughs, which a lion could reach. The males stayed together on the ground, dancing, shouting, bristling, baring teeth.

A healthy cat would never have attacked through those thorns, but this one, unable to hunt or even drive the hyenas off the kills of others, no longer had a choice. Maddened by the scent of meat, he flayed himself as his forepaws

199

scooped away the thorn wall.

"Oh, no; oh, no!" Jerry gasped. Once inside, even though he was crippled and bleeding, the beast would still overmatch ten or twelve little men with no better weapons than chipped pebbles and stone-whittled sticks. He'd scarcely stop at killing one. No, he'd lay about him, pile high the corpses, then gorge and sleep, gorge and sleep, while sunlight slashed across the women and children in their tree, besieged.

Jerry, almost in shock, knew that he was back on the ground and that he couldn't just do nothing while the thing happened, whatever it cost him.

He felt strangely cool, as if he stood in the moonlight, apart from his body, watching and directing it according to calculation:

Poke the fire, throw on more fuel, build a goodly blaze. Take three or four long sticks, thrust them into the coals, whip them in the air till they are fluttering torches. Hold that bundle in your left hand, the hardened spear in your right. Run forward to meet the lion.

He is almost through the thorn wall but has

stopped his assault to stare warily in your direction. Lightning or the friction of wind-rubbed brush must kindle grass fires often enough, devastatingly enough, that animals have a built-in dread of flame. As you come near, the bleeding lion snarls and crouches. How big are those fangs!

From the ape-folk, sudden utter stillness. White under the moon, the skull regards you from its pole.

Mowgli act, drifts crazily across your head. "Take that, Lame Thief!"—though your outside observer knows the poor creature is only trying to survive—and you ram your torch bundle at the great maw.

Be careful. Let him make a determined advance, and you're done. You'll go down beneath a swipe of claws that can break a neck with one blow. Your fire will go out forever. Keep the man-eater in retreat. Yell, chatter, show teeth. Thrust also with your right hand that carries the spear. Ha, blood spurts out!

With a final rumble from deep in his throat, more sigh than challenge, the lame lion drags himself off into the night to die.

For a long while, Jerry stared into the murk behind the thorns. He knew he must show stark in the sight of those eyes. His torches guttered low, became embers. Silence and cold flowed back around him.

Trembling racked his frame. He retreated to his place beneath the tree, stoked his fire, and settled down to wait out the night, sobbing, now, with the terror he had refused to feel as he drove away the lion.

After the jubilation and the first blurted brief account and the medical care for minor hurts, Antonio Viana took his nephew home and put him to bed. Several hours' sleep did wonders. Awakening toward evening, Jerry learned that a family feast was being prepared to celebrate his safe return.

His uncle led him to the study and offered him a glass of sherry. "No, thank you," the boy said, but he appreciated the compliment. To a Spaniard, the offer was a tribute to the manhood he had shown.

Antonio smiled and gave him a soft drink instead, then filled a wineglass, and lit a cigar for himself. They settled into creaky old leather chairs that still smelled faintly of horses. Books surrounded them, save where a window gave on dusk and multitudinous twinkling lights. A warm breeze carried in odors of jasmine.

"Well," the scientist said with a smile, "we relax before dinner, we two, no? Maybe we can talk over what happened in more detail. Your aunt and cousins, you must see them, of course —and tomorrow the anthropologists—but there will be so much excitement, I think you will want to take this chance to arrange your thoughts."

"I suppose so." Jerry frowned at the ice that tinkled in his glass. "But I'm—well—I'm happy to be back, that's all."

"Understood. However, in retrospect, at least, your experience was fascinating."

"Kind of rough." Jerry grimaced. "I don't mean the being, uh, marooned. Sure, I'm glad to know I had the guts to survive, but those . . . pithecanthropuses . . . those little monsters. . . . I don't like to think about them. Cannibals and—"

"Oh?" Antonio raised dark brows. "Yet you rescued them."

"Yeah. I don't know why."

"What makes you think they were cannibals?"

"Huh?" Jerry needed a moment to get over astonishment. "I told you; they attacked me to kill."

"How could you expect them to know you were human? In fact, you were not, from their viewpoint." Antonio smiled through his beard. "As an American might say, oddness works both ways." More seriously: "You have told how the males—no, I will say the men—were prepared to die for their women and children. Why should they be, unless they loved them?"

"But that skull—like a trophy!"

"Someone they slew? Or someone who died but was revered?" Antonio paused before he added, "Remember how Catholics preserve the relics of saints. I think those people of the dawn already had souls, Jerry. And they endured; they actually found the strength to love. Be proud of such forebears."

The boy spoke no word, because at that moment a glory was opening for him.

His uncle reached to clasp his shoulder. "And they," he said simply, "could be proud of their descendant."

Gone. Gone.

You send stranger, Old Father? Stranger *is* Old Father?

Light, wind, ripple, rustle across grasses. Clouds scud. Antelope race cloud shadows. Wings, wings, wings.

Stranger gone. Lame lion gone.

Sour gray ashes. Warm on palm of hand. Prod with stick like stranger. Blow like stranger. Puff-ff-ff; tiny flames. Put on dry stick. Slow, careful, careful. Not to anger Old Father.

Touch stranger's spear?

Spear out of fire? Spear dark from fire, from blood of lion?

For shes, for cubs—grab spear! Lift! Shout, dance under morning sun!

Hard, sharp, black spear. Make many. Kill big beasts. No more hungry.

Fire. Light in moonless night. Scare off lion,

hyena. Harden spear, spear, spear, spear, spear.
Make man band strong!

Thank you, Old Father. This holy fire you
have given us—we must never let it die.

THE TRUTH OF IT

by Barry N. Malzberg

GREG VII HAD A SURPRISE in store for him when he asked the command robot how much longer the journey to Sirius would take. The machine told him the truth.

"I may as well," it said, rather sadly. "I can't conceal this forever, you know, and it might as well be a young boy who hears it first; perhaps they'll take it better if it comes from you. You see, I'm afraid it's never going to end—the trip, I mean. I seem to have made a mistake with the charts and the galactic compass, and, well, we're

207

completely lost. I don't think we're even in the same galaxy anymore, and we're just going to keep on traveling. I'm terribly embarrassed."

"But I thought it was only a few months!" Greg VII said, with some irritation. He was only twelve, and he was scheduled to be among the first generation that would enjoy its full adolescence in the Sirius system; hence his loss of control could be forgiven. He had been looking forward to "growing up among the stars," which was the way the elders put it. "That's what you've been telling everybody!"

"Yes," the command robot said. It was fitted with a speaker and diaphragm, which enabled it, despite the fact that it was merely a machine, to sound quite lifelike. "I know. I admit that I've been lying. It's time to come out with the truth, however." It made a sound vaguely like throat-clearing. "As I say, I can't conceal the truth indefinitely. You break the news to them; make it your responsibility. It's all a terrible mistake, but the ship is self-sustaining, as you know, thanks to the recycling gear and the hydroponics, so no one's really in any danger. You'll just have

a rather boring life. But then," the machine said plaintively, "consider my position."

"It's not fair!" Greg VII said angrily and, having nothing more to say to the robot, left the rather dim room in which it was housed. It was a shame, that was all. He had been looking forward to the Sirius system and the excitement of being one of the youngest in the first large colony to be set up in a new system; instead, it turned out that the stupid machine had gotten lost. What were they supposed to do, all two hundred of them, live in the ship forever? He guessed that was what the machine had been suggesting.

"You know what?" Greg VII said to his father somewhat later, having temporarily forgotten his anger at the machine in a game of null-gravity gymnastics. "You know what the robot told me today? That it had gotten us lost, and that we were *never* going to get to Sirius, because it missed the galaxy compass or something. We're just going to run in space forever."

"Is that so?" his father said pleasantly. He was a biologist, one of the five responsible for the hydroponics, and nearly always preoccupied, what with his mind on carbon dioxide ratios. "That's very interesting."

"You know, Greg, you must learn to tell the truth," his mother said, on her way back to the cleansing cubicle with the used eating gear. "We don't mind a little habit like making things up, but people of your own age won't be so understanding, once we get to Sirius and start the colonist's hard life—"

"But I'm not lying," Greg VII said. "It's the truth. I went and asked the machine when we were going to land, and it said never. I didn't make it up. It's not my fault! The machine apologized to me, as a matter of fact."

Greg's father stood up from the table, exchanged a look with his wife, then shook his head and sighed. "Your mother is right, son," he said. "You really shouldn't lie, even to your family, as a way of making conversation. It's a bad habit, and you're twelve years old now, which is very close to having real responsibilities." He looked at his hands wearily, then at Greg. "I guess I should spank you or something," he said doubtfully, "but I'm not up to it."

"You see, Greg," his mother said, setting aside the eating gear and kneeling before him, "it isn't that we want to hurt or frighten you, but when you go to start a new life near a new sun, traveling for years and years in a big ship to get there, there's so much at stake that you've got to try— well, try not to be twelve years old." She wiped her hands and put them lightly on his knees. Both of his parents were gentle people, although Greg could see that they were upset. "Do you understand us?"

"It's not a lie," Greg VII said. "It's not a lie, and the machine told the truth, and it apologized to me, and you'll see. You'll see!" His voice grew shrill as his father approached to punish him.

And the ship, carried by the unlimited power of a thousand engines, continued on its endless perigee—past Sirius, past Aldebaran, past the Orion constellation itself, and at cross angles to the Milky Way—and made, dead on target, toward the outer edges of the universe, where, for all we know, it may now be, although Greg, now fifty-five, is too preoccupied with the ship's government to wonder.

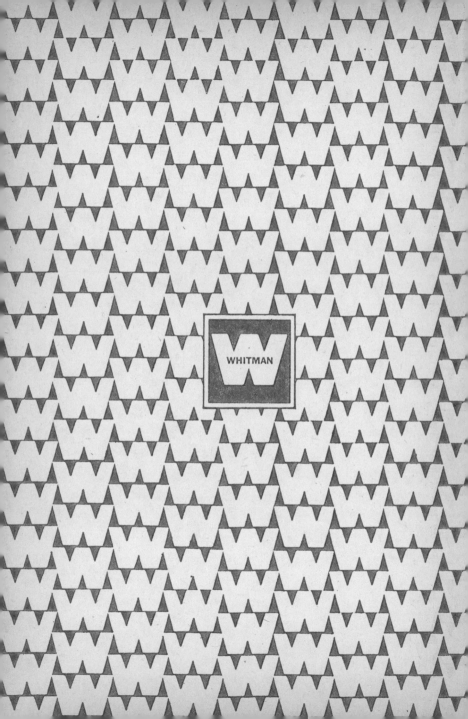